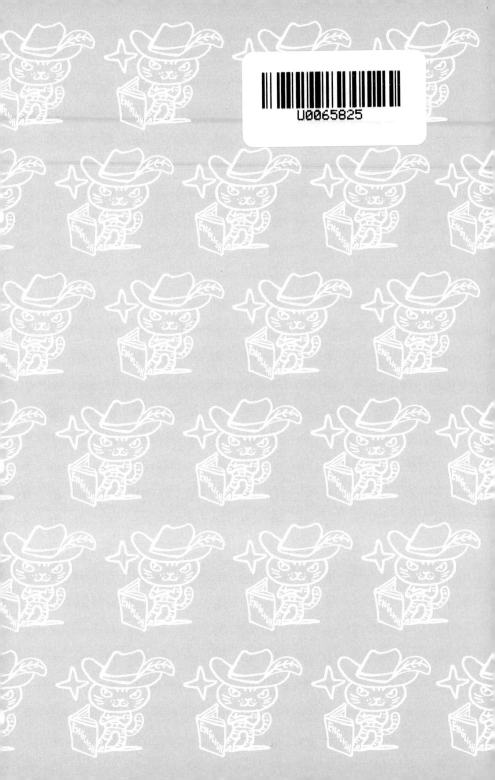

U0065825

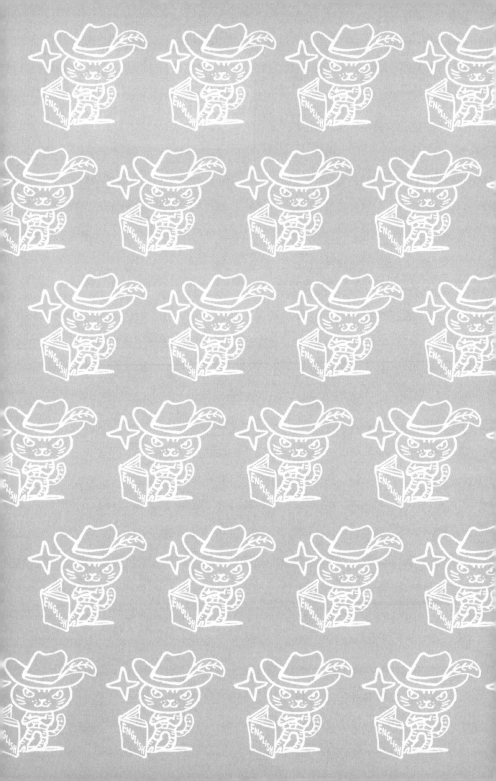

準備→練習→應考→滿分一氣呵成，
34招取分技巧，完美攻略多益4大聽力題型，
只要聽出關鍵字句，就能秒選正確答案！

何謂 TOEIC® L&R TEST ？

TOEIC測驗為測試英語溝通能力的一項測驗，由位於美國的非營利測驗開發機構Educational Testing Service(ETS)開發製作。測驗結果是以分數表示，而非以合格、不合格表示。

目前TOEIC測驗有測試「聽」、「讀」能力的TOEIC® Listening & Reading Test（TOEIC L&R測驗），及測試「說」、「寫」能力的TOEIC® Speaking & Writing Tests（TOEIC S&W測驗）二種。

測試「聽」、「讀」能力的TOEIC® Listening & Reading Test，分為聽力部分（100題／約45分鐘）與閱讀部分（100題／75分鐘），是項需在約2小時內以畫卡方式回答總計200題的測驗。

關於聽力部分

TOEIC® Listening & Reading Test的聽力部分，需在約45分鐘內回答100題。2016年5月時有部分題目構成有所變更，各PART題目數量的分配與過往不同，而且內容也有部分變更，比如加入了3人對話、需同時參照圖表作答的問題以及詢問意圖的問題等等。

測驗播放的錄音，會由美國、英國、加拿大、澳洲的錄音員負責收錄。

聽力部分的構成

PART	PART名稱	題目數
PART 1	照片描述 Photographs	6
PART 2	應答問題 Questions	25
PART 3	簡短會話 Conversations	39（3小題×13大題）
PART 4	簡短獨白 Talks	30（3小題×10大題）

關於聽力部分的4個PART

PART 1　照片描述 Photographs（6題）

　　試題本上僅印有照片，關於照片的4個敘述只會播放一次，需從4個敘述中，選出最適當描述照片的句子。

PART 2　應答問題 Questions（25題）

　　針對1個人的發言或提問，會播放3句應答，僅會播放一次。需從3句應答中，選出回覆最為適當的選項。題目及選項皆無印於試題本，僅以錄音播放。

PART 3　簡短會話 Conversations（39題）

　　對話只會播放一次，採取聽完對話之後接著回答3題的形式。需聽取13題分的對話，回答總計39個問題。

2016年5月測驗改制後，新加入①聽完3人對話後作答的問題、②詢問＂　＂部分意圖的問題、③參照圖表作答的問題。

試題本上僅印有題目、選項及圖表，未印有會話。

PART 4　簡短獨白 Talks（30題）

會播放一次電話語音留言、會議內容節錄、廣播（通知）等說明，採取聽完說明後接著回答3題的形式。共需聽取10題份的說明，回答總計30個問題。

2016年5月測驗改制後，新加入①詢問＂　　＂部分意圖的問題、②參照圖表作答的問題。

試題本上僅印有題目、選項及圖表，未印有會話。

User's Guide
本書的 **使用說明**

本書是由TOEIC測驗PART1、2、3、4（聽力部分）的攻略技巧，以及仿造正式考試編寫的模擬試題所構成。首先請閱讀各PART的攻略技巧，掌握答題的訣竅，之後再計時挑戰模擬考。

Step 1. 了解TOEIC測驗的基礎！

TOEIC測驗，尤其是聽力部分的概要從P005起有所解說，可由此快速掌握整體的狀況。

何謂 TOEIC® L&R TEST？

TOEIC測驗為測試英語溝通能力的一項測驗，由位於美國的非營利測驗開發機構Educational Testing Service(ETS)開發製作。測驗結果是以分數表示，而非以合格、不合格表示。

目前TOEIC測驗有測試「聽」、「讀」能力的TOEIC® Listening & Reading Test（TOEIC L&R測驗），及測試「說」、「寫」能力的TOEIC® Speaking & Writing Tests（TOEIC S&W測驗）二種。

測試「聽」、「讀」能力的TOEIC® Listening & Reading Test，分為聽力部分（100題／約45分鐘）與閱讀部分（100題／75分鐘），是一項需在2小時內以畫卡方式回答總計200題的測驗。

關於聽力部分

TOEIC® Listening & Reading Test的聽力部分，需在約45分鐘內回答100題。2016年5月時有部分題目構成有所變更，各PART題目數量的分配與這些不同，而且內容也有部分變更，比如加入了3人對話、需同時參照圖表作答的問題以及詢問意圖的問題等等。

測驗播放的錄音，會由美國、英國、加拿大、澳洲的錄音員負責收錄。

聽力部分的構成

PART	PART名稱	題目數
PART 1	照片描述 Photographs	6
PART 2	應答問題 Questions	25
PART 3	簡短會話 Conversations	39（3小題×13大題）
PART 4	簡短獨白 Talks	30（3小題×10大題）

關於聽力部分的4個PART

PART 1　照片描述 Photographs（6題）

試題本上僅印有照片，關於照片的4個敘述只會播放一次，需從4個敘述中，選出最適當描述照片的句子。

PART 2　應答問題 Questions（25題）

針對1個人的發言或提問，會播放3句應答，僅會播放一次。需從3句應答中，選出回覆最為適當的選項。題目及選項皆無印於試題本，僅以錄音播放。

PART 3　簡短會話 Conversations（39題）

對話只會播放一次，採取聽完對話之後接著回答3題的形式。需聽取13題分的對話，回答總計39個問題。

Step2. 學習聽力部分的攻略法！

本部分將解説各PART的攻略法。請於此學習作答的訣竅，例如聽錄音時要注意聽哪裡等等。

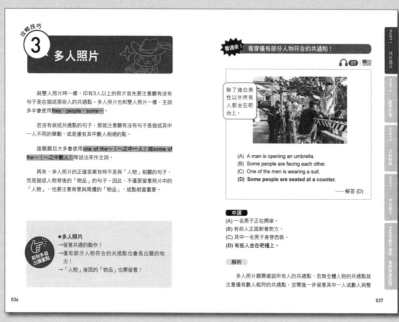

利用練習題確認學到的技巧

Step3. 確認必背常出英文單字！

　　此部分將各PART經常出現的英文單字整理成檢視表，請記得最少最少也要背下這些單字喔。

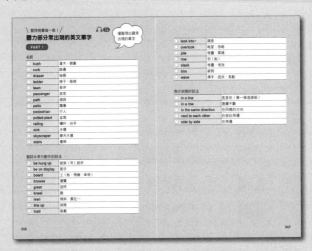

Step4. 挑戰模擬試題！

　　此部分刊載了聽力部分1回合的模擬試題，請當成正式考試應考，集中精神作答。P176開始有詳細的解說、解答及中譯。

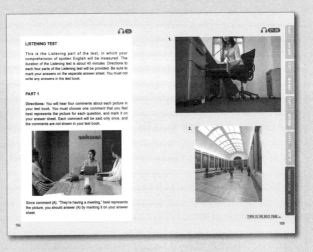

關於本書音檔

　　本書附有音檔連結，其中收錄PART1、2攻略技巧中刊載的例題、練習題以及模擬試題的錄音內容。

　　有錄音的題目寫有音軌編號，內容與TOEIC正式考試一樣以4國發音進行錄音。

🎧 **01** ⋯⋯音軌編號

🇺🇸 ⋯⋯美國發音

🇬🇧 ⋯⋯英國發音

🇨🇦 ⋯⋯加拿大發音

🇦🇺 ⋯⋯澳洲發音

　　全書音檔請掃描QR code或由以下網址下載MP3形式的音檔至你的電腦裡。下載至電腦後，請使用播放軟體播放。

本書MP3 QR code

★ 因各家手機系統不同，若無法直接掃描，仍可以電腦連結網址https://reurl.cc/qe7DD雲端下載收聽）

3 步驟手機隨掃下載音檔

step1. 從您的手機中找出QR code條碼掃描APP

step2. 對準書中的QR code條碼內容

step3. 進入MP3音檔的雲端連結，即可下載

Preface
前言

從我開始考多益算起已經15年了，在東京的八重洲開教室授課也過了13個年頭，在這期間課程一直都廣受商業人士歡迎，半數以上的學生都是經口耳相傳前來參加的。

2016年5月TOEIC測驗改制以來，每個PART都變難了，就連聽力部分（PART1～4）也不例外。尤其是PART 2，開始會出些較貼近現實應答的題目，無法順利取得高分的人似乎也不在少數。

因此在本書中，將會運用在我的課堂當中受到好評的得分法，詳細解説PART 2的攻略方式。

正因為這是令多數人感到棘手的PART，所以只要能夠在這部分得高分，便能成為很大的武器。希望你務必透過本書掌握訣竅，將其變成你的得分源。

PART 1、3、4也在改制之後出了全新類型的題目，多了一些除了聽力之外還需具備閱讀能力才能夠得分的題目。

雖然加強基礎能力最為重要，但要想提升分數，掌握答題的竅門及出題的習慣也是不可或缺的。

希望各位能盡可能利用捷徑提高分數，因此本書中寫有大量的小提示。祈願你能參考本書，盡早達成你的目標分數。

Contents
目錄

Part 1 照片描述

Part 2 應答問題

Part

3

簡短對話

Part 4 簡短獨白

TOEIC聽力測驗　預想模擬試題

PART 1

照片描述

試題本上只有印照片，會播放關於
照片的4個敘述句，需在4個敘述中
選出最符合照片的一個。

PART 1 概要

題數 6題

作答時間 每題約5秒

題型範例 試題本上只印有照片。聽完4個敘述句後,從中選出1個與照片內容相符的句子。敘述句僅以聲音播放,不會印在試題本上。

↑
正式考試時,每頁會印有2張大大的照片。由於試題本上沒有題目及選項,所以全部聽完後再選出正確答案。

答案卡

1.　Ⓐ　Ⓑ　Ⓒ　Ⓓ

↑

共有6題，皆為4個選項。

錄音範例　請由4個敘述中，選出最符合照片內容的1個。

(A)　One of the hikers is pushing a bicycle.
(B)　Two people are walking along a path.
(C)　Trees are being planted in a forest.
(D)　Two people are walking in opposite directions.

PART 1 最簡單

重點在預先看好照片

　　2016年5月試題改制後，PART 1從10題縮減成6題。先聽完4個敘述，再從中選出作為試題本上的照片描述最為適當的1個。描述句僅以聲音播放，且每句只唸一次。因此，一定得在聲音開始播放前先看好照片。

　　題目的類型有不少種，首先就先來認識一下整體共通該注意的地方。

照片中有「人」的時候

　　要快速確認動作、身上穿戴的東西及背景等等。

照片中是「物品」或「風景」的時候

　　要快速確認物品為何、位置關係、排列方式及數量等等。除了椅子、電腦、圖畫、車子、建築物等物品外，也會出現公園、海、河川等風景的照片。照片中出現的所有東西都要確認。

● 無法從照片上判斷，只能用想像的句子，或是描述到照片上沒有的東西的句子，都不要選。

● 留意時態也很重要。
　　正確答案大多是「現在進行式」或「現在式的被動語態」。其中，傳達人物動作的照片，現在進行式的句子為正確答案的情形最多。

　　另一方面，**物品或風景照片**的正確答案就以「**現在完成式的被動語態**」或「現在式的被動語態」居多。

　　此外，表達狀態的照片，正確答案有可能是現在式，且題目也有可能將There is/are開頭的句子設計成正確答案。

● 要小心換句話說的表達方式。比如：

　　‧印有雜誌的照片用的不是magazine，而是reading materials
　　‧使用merchandise、item來取代具體的物品
　　‧握手的照片不說shaking hands，而說greeting
　　‧海邊的照片不用seaside，而是用water

　　諸如此類。除了上述例子外，還有各式各樣的代換説法會被用來出題。

攻略技巧 1 單人照片

　　首先，要注意播放的英文主詞、動詞和接續的敘述等是否與照片一致。

　　PART 1的人物照片題中，描述該人物動作的句子壓倒性居多，在這種情況下，「現在進行式的英文」常為正確答案，在整個PART 1中，正確答案是現在進行式的就佔7～8成。

　　非描述動作而是描述人物狀態或人物位置關係的句子，除了「現在進行式」以外，「現在式」、「現在完成式」以及三種時態的「被動語態」也可能會是正確答案。

新制多益出題重點

●描述人物「動作」的句子
→正確答案很高機率就是現在進行式的句子！

●描述人物「狀態」或「位置關係」的句子
→不僅現在進行式，現在式、現在完成式、被動語態也可能是正確答案！

PART 1 照片描述

PART 2 應答問題

PART 3 簡短對話

PART 4 簡短獨白

TOEIC聽力測驗 預想模擬試題

看過來！ 描述人物「動作」的照片要注意「動詞」！

表示「觀看玻璃櫥窗」這個動作的動詞不一定會直接出現在選項中。

(A) She is standing in front of a glass case.

(B) She is entering a supermarket.

(C) She is looking into a box.

不要漏聽各個選項的動詞！

(D) She is going to make some cakes.

——解答 (A)

中譯

(A) 她正站在玻璃櫥櫃前。

(B) 她正走進超市。

(C) 她正在往一個盒子裡看。

(D) 她正要去做點蛋糕。

解析

這是張呈現女性動作的照片。這位女性正在觀看玻璃櫥窗，但直接描述這個動作的句子She is looking into a glass case.（她正

在觀看玻璃櫥窗。）卻不在選項之中。雖然有(C) She is looking into a box.，但那位女性看的並非盒子，所以這個選項是錯的。合乎該位女性動作的是(A) 她正站在玻璃櫥櫃前，因此正確答案是(A)。當題目的照片是呈現動作的時候，最重要的便是注意使用的動詞，且迅速找到與照片動作相符的動詞。

如本例這樣照片中僅有1人的題目，照片中若為女性，那麼正確答案的句子主詞大多會是she或a [the] woman，若為男性則以he或a [the] man開頭居多，這就是答題關鍵。

看過來！ 也要注意人物「身上穿戴的物品」！

 🎧 **03**

並非正在搬運 a laptop computer（筆記型電腦）。

並非正在用mobile phone（手機）講電話。

(A) He's wearing a necktie.
(B) He's carrying a laptop computer.
(C) He's talking on his mobile phone.
(D) He's reading a newspaper.

——解答 (A)

(A) 他繫著領帶。

(B) 他正在搬運一台筆記型電腦。

(C) 他正在講電話。

(D) 他正在讀報紙。

解析

　　除了「動作」以外也可能會問到「身上的物品」，所以請留意「動作」＋「身上的物品」。就動作來說，男性雖然打開了(B) a laptop computer（筆記型電腦），但是並不是在搬運它。另外，他也不是用mobile phone（手機）在講電話，所以(C)和照片也不相符。不過(A)的「繫著領帶（a necktie）」就與照片一致。

　　單人照片中，當未出現表示該人物動作的英文時，正確答案多半是敘述那個人身上穿戴的物品的句子。在確認照片的時候，記得也要留意眼鏡、帽子、安全帽、領帶、包包等穿戴在該人物身上的物品。

也要注意人與物品的「位置關係」！

 04

詢問人與物品的「位置關係」

(A) A woman is standing in front of a sofa.
(B) A woman is sitting beside a projector.
(C) A woman is seated next to a potted plant.
(D) A woman is working at her desk.

——解答 (C)

中譯

(A) 一名女性正站在沙發前。
(B) 一名女性正坐在投影機旁。
(C) 一名女性坐在盆栽旁邊。
(D) 一名女性正在書桌前工作。

解析

　　照片中的女性正坐在盆栽旁。描述「坐著」這個照片中的動作的英文是(B)和(C)，但確切敘述出人物動作以及人與物品的位置關

係的是(C)「一名女性坐在盆栽旁邊。」。

(B)是使用is sitting來表示「坐著」這個動作，而(C)則是使用is seated，利用seat（使就坐）來表現。表示人與物品之間「位置關係」的英文被用來出題時，大多會使用next to ～（在～旁邊）之類描述位置的表達，所以如果有這樣的表達，就要在「人物」動作外再多留意其與「物品」間的位置關係。

那麼，現在就再來作作看1題使用單人照片出題的題目吧。
請播放錄音Track 05。

請聽錄音作答

練習問題 1

注意「女性的動作」和與「樹木」的位置關係！

(A) Some trees have been stacked by a road.
(B) A woman is leaning against a fence.
(C) Some trees are being sprayed with water.
(D) A woman is reading beneath a tree.

(A) 有些樹木被堆在路邊。
(B) 一名女性正倚靠在圍欄旁。
(C) 有些樹正在被澆水。
(D) 一名女性正在樹下看書。

正解 (D)

　　照片中女性正坐在樹下看書。這張照片裡最醒目的是正在看書的女性與樹，別只關注女性的動作，只要連女性與樹木間的位置關係也一起留意去聽，就會發現正確答案是(D)「一名女性正在樹下看書」。

註釋

□ stack 堆疊
□ lean against 倚靠在～
□ spray 噴灑

攻略技巧

2 雙人照片

　　雙人照片的情況，需留意**2人共通的動作、其中1人的動作以及身上穿戴的「物品」**等。另外，那2人正在進行怎樣的動作之類的細節也是需注意的要點。

　　舉例來說，就是2人正在握手、正面對面坐著或是正比鄰而坐這類描述。

　　在那類照片之中，主詞大多會使用**they、some people、one of the ～、two of the people、the (two) men或the (two) women**等。

新制多益
出題重點

● **雙人照片**
→留意2人共通的動作、其中1人的動作和身上穿戴的「物品」！

● **描述人物「狀態」或「位置關係」的句子**
→也要注意2人之間的位置關係！

也要注意人與物品的「位置關係」！

2人手上都拿
著文件
→共通的動作

(A) The women are making a cup of coffee.

(B) One of the women is giving a speech.

(C) One of the women is returning some merchandise.

(D) The women are holding some documents.

──解答　(D)

中譯

(A) 幾位女性正在泡咖啡。

(B) 其中一名女性正在演講。

(C) 其中一名女性正在歸還一些商品。

(D) 幾位女性正拿著一些文件。

解析

　　雙人照片中，首先要看的是共通的動作。照片中2人手上都拿著文件，所以(D)「幾位女性正拿著一些文件」是正確答案。

　　本例為2人有共通動作的照片，但有時也會出將焦點放在其中1人的行動上的題目，那種題目中經常會使用one of the ～（～之中的1人）這種表達。

 注意2人的「位置關係」

有2位人物登場，但並無共通的動作。
→也要留意2人的位置關係

(A) A woman is watering some flowers.
(B) There is a reception desk behind a man.
(C) A man is getting into an elevator.
(D) There are some documents on a counter.

——解答　(B)

中譯

(A) 一名女性正在澆花。

(B) 男子後面有一個接待櫃台。

(C) 一名男子正走進電梯。

(D) 桌子上有一些文件。

解析

　　照片中可在男性背後看見一個接待櫃台，只要將男性與櫃檯的位置關係納入考慮，(B)「男子後面有一個接待櫃台」就與照片相符。以There is/are起頭的句子也常被用在正確選項中。

　　照片正中央印有人物時，容易只留意那個人的動作和身上穿戴的物品，但有時也會發生描述背景中物品的句子才是正確答案的情形，也就是以背景中的「物品」為主詞，描寫其狀態的句子才是正確答案的這種模式。因此，不光是照片中的「人物」，連背景、周遭的「物品」也一定要注意。

　接下來，就再來作作看1題使用雙人照片出題的題目吧。

練習問題 2

注意2人的動作及
與導覽板之間的位
置關係

(A) A bicycle is leaning against a tree.
(B) Cyclists have stopped in front of a sign.
(C) A bicycle is being repaired.
(D) A group of people is planting some trees.

(A) 一輛腳踏車靠在一顆樹上。
(B) 腳踏車騎士們停在一個標示前。
(C) 一輛腳踏車正在進行修理。
(D) 一群人正在種樹。

正確答案 (B)

　　照片中2人都在看導覽板,因此描述了2人的動作以及與導覽板之間的位置關係的(B)是正確答案。正式考試時會有像是只有腳踏車的照片、騎著腳踏車的人的照片、詢問腳踏車與其他物品的位置關係的照片等等,出題的方式相當多樣化。

註釋

- ☐ lean against 倚靠在～
- ☐ cyclist 腳踏車騎士
- ☐ in front of 在前面
- ☐ repair 修理

3 多人照片

　　與雙人照片時一樣，印有3人以上的照片首先要注意聽有沒有句子是在描述那些人的共通點。多人照片也和雙人照片一樣，主詞多半會使用they、people、some～。

　　若沒有敘述共通點的句子，那就注意聽有沒有句子是描述其中一人不同的舉動，或是僅有其中數人相通的點。

　　這類題目大多會使用one of the～（～之中一人）或some of the～（～之中數人）等説法來作主詞。

　　再來，多人照片的正確答案有時不是與「人物」相關的句子，而是描述人物背後的「物品」的句子。因此，不僅要留意照片中的「人物」，也要注意背景與周遭的「物品」，這點相當重要。

新制多益
出題重點

●多人照片

→留意共通的動作！

→僅有部分人物符合的共通點也會是出題的地方！

→「人物」後面的「物品」也需留意！

看過來！ **看穿僅有部分人物符合的共通點！**

 09

除了這位男性以外所有人都坐在吧台上。

(A) A man is opening an umbrella.
(B) Some people are facing each other.
(C) One of the men is wearing a suit.
(D) Some people are seated at a counter.

——解答 (D)

中譯

(A) 一名男子正在開傘。
(B) 有些人正面對著對方。
(C) 其中一名男子身穿西裝。
(D) 有些人坐在吧檯上。

解析

　　多人照片題需確認所有人的共通點，若無全體人物的共通點就注意僅有數人相符的共通點，並需進一步留意其中一人或數人與整

體的相異之處。在本題之中，描述出照片內僅有數人相同之處的 (D)「有些人坐在吧檯上」即為正確答案。

 有時「背景」也會是出題處

🎧 10 🇬🇧

廣場上聚集著許多人。

→描述「人」的句子不一定是正確答案！

→「背景」也要多加留意！

(A) Some workers are arranging tables at a cafe.
(B) A staircase is adjacent to a fountain.
(C) A woman is setting up a large umbrella.
(D) Some buildings are located behind a plaza.

——解答 (D)

中譯

(A) 有些工作人員正在一間咖啡店排桌子。

(B) 一個階梯緊臨著一個噴泉。

(C) 一名女性正在架設一支大型的傘。

(D) 有些建築物坐落在廣場的後方。

解析

　　雖說視線會不自覺地看向照片中央的遮陽傘和周遭人們的動作，但有時描述背景的句子才是正確答案。在確認照片時，請記得也要看看背景。這題的正確答案也是敘述背景的(D)「有些建築物坐落在廣場的後方」。雖說(A)用了工作人員、(C)用了女性當作主詞，但句子卻未正確描述他們的動作。此外，照片中並未拍到噴水池，所以(B)也是錯的。

4 物品或風景照片

若是物品照片，就需注意物品的狀態、位置關係和排列方式。

正確答案的句子，如果主詞是物品，那麼動詞大多都是被動語態，不過視動詞而定有時也會是主動語態。另外，There is/are開頭的句子也可能會是正確答案。

新制多益出題重點

● 物品或風景照片
→留意物品的「狀態」、「位置關係」和「排列右式」！
→主詞是物品時，動詞大多為「被動語態」。

這裡就來介紹一些陳列著建築物、車子和腳踏車等物品的照片中，經常使用的單字和說法。

物品照片中經常使用的動詞

● set 放置
● arrange 安排
● face 面對
● hang 懸掛、吊起
● display 展示
● line up 排隊

表示位置關係的說法

- in a row 連續不斷
- next to 在～旁邊
- along 沿著
- above 在～上面

- side by side 並排
- in front of 在～之前
- under 在～下面
- by 在～旁邊

看過來！ 留意物品的「狀態」！

curb（路緣）
在照片描述題
中很常出現！

(A) Some cars have been parked alongside a curb.

(B) Some cars are being pushed into a truck.

(C) A car door is being closed.

(D) An airplane is being loaded with luggage.

——解答 (A)

中譯

(A) 有些車停在路邊。

(B) 有些車正被推到貨車上。

(C) 車門正被關上。

(D) 一輛飛機正在裝載行李。

解析

　　車子的照片很常出現，通常是詢問其狀態或排列方式，不過若有拍到人物，就也可能會問到人的動作，所以必須多加注意。這張照片的正確答案是(A)「有些車停在路邊。」，而且curb（路邊）一詞是TOEIC的必背單字。

　　在風景照片中，需留意那是個怎樣的地方，以及那裡有什麼東西。公園、高樓大廈、海邊或河邊等水邊也很常出題。

　　此外，有時候正確答案並非是僅描述部分畫面中央物品的句子，而是敘述背景物品的句子，所以照片的背景也需仔細確認。

看過來！ 留意物品間的「位置關係」

 12

注意「卡車」與「土」的位置關係！

(A) A truck is being parked in a parking garage.

(B) There's a pile of earth behind a truck.

(C) Some merchandise is being loaded into a truck.

(D) Some workers are landscaping a property.

——解答 (B)

中譯

(A) 一輛貨車正停入在停車庫裡。

(B) 在貨車後面有一堆土。

(C) 貨車正在裝載一些商品。

(D) 有些工人正在替一座建物造景。

照片中印有一台卡車，其後的地面上堆積著土壤，正確答案即是表示卡車與積土之間位置關係的(B)。這裡使用earth這個單字來表示積土，所以可能有人會因此弄錯。選項中有3個使用到truck，因此得聽出哪個是正確敘述卡車狀態的句子才有辦法作答。

接下來，就再來做做看1題以物品或風景照片來出題的題目吧。

練習問題 3 13

沒有拍到「人物」
→詢問「物品」的
位置關係！

(A) A fence around a swimming pool is being painted.
(B) Some chairs are arranged side by side.
(C) An umbrella is being set up beside a pool.
(D) A towel has been placed on each of the chairs.

(A) 在游泳池旁的圍籬正在進行油漆。
(B) 有些椅子被併置在一起。
(C) 一隻雨傘被架在游泳池旁。
(D) 每個椅子上都各放有一條毛巾。

正確答案　(B)

　　由於沒有拍到人物，所以可能會認為題目會問及椅子或泳池的
位置關係或排列方式。排列著物品（本題中是椅子）的照片，正確
答案多半是聚焦在排列方式上的句子，本題也一樣，正確答案為
(B)。排列著車子或椅子等物品時，使用side by side（並排列著）
這種說法的情形十分常見。

　　另外，side by side在雙人照片中也很常會使用。

註釋

☐ fence 圍籬　　　☐ arrange 安排
☐ set up 設立、設置　☐ towel 毛巾
☐ place 放置

聽力部分常出現的英文單字

🎧 14

僅整理出最常出現的單字

PART 1

名詞

☐ bush	灌木、樹叢
☐ curb	路邊
☐ drawer	抽屜
☐ ladder	梯子、階梯
☐ lawn	草坪
☐ passenger	旅客
☐ path	道路
☐ patio	露臺
☐ pedestrian	行人
☐ potted plant	盆栽
☐ railing	欄杆、扶手
☐ sink	水槽
☐ skyscraper	摩天大樓
☐ stairs	樓梯

動詞＆表示動作的說法

☐ be hung up	被掛（吊）起來
☐ be on display	展示
☐ board	上（船、飛機、車等）
☐ browse	瀏覽
☐ greet	招呼
☐ kneel	跪
☐ lean	傾斜、靠在～
☐ line up	排隊
☐ load	裝載

☐	look into~	調查
☐	overlook	眺望、忽略
☐	pile	堆疊、累積
☐	row	划（船）
☐	stack	堆疊、堆放
☐	trim	修剪
☐	wave	揮手、起扶、晃動

表示狀態的說法

☐	in a line	直直地（像一條直線般）
☐	in a row	連續不斷
☐	in the same direction	在同樣的方向
☐	next to each other	在彼此旁邊
☐	side by side	在旁邊

PART 2

應答問題

針對1個人的發言或提問，會播放3句應答，需在3句應答中選出最適切的選項。題目及選項皆無印於試題本，僅以錄音播放。

PART 2 概要

題數 25題

作答時間 每題約5秒

題型範例 試題本

> 7. Mark your answer on your answer sheet.

↑
試題本上只有寫這樣。
題目、選項都沒寫,必須全部聽完之後,再選出正確答案。

答案卡

> 7.　(A)　(B)　(C)

錄音範例

> Are you familiar with the new software application?
>
> (A) Over 20 people have applied.
> (B) Both employees and their families can join.
> (C) I've just finished the training program.

↑
從3個選項中選出適當的答案。

不少題目即便聽得懂也會猶豫該選哪個

在2016年5月試題改制之後，聽力部分的PART 2由30題縮減成25題，不過內容上困難的題目卻增加了，這是由於題目和選項都必須用聽的的題目變多了的關係。

此外，雖然後頭才會再詳加說明，不過正確答案是使用間接回應而非直接回應的題目數量變多了。而且，會讓非母語者感到問答之間有些距離的回覆才是正確答案的情況也增加，明明題目和選項都聽得懂，卻會煩惱「所以哪個才是正確答案啊？」的這種出題方式多了不少。

舉例來說，如果是在5～6年前，就有許多即使沒有將選項一個一個仔細聽完也能靠技巧、訣竅來作答的題目，像是以where或when等5W1H的疑問詞起頭的情況下，若題目的開頭是where就只要專心聽地點，若題目以when起頭就只要專心聽日期、時間即可等等。

但是，由於現在很多時候是問答間有點距離的間接回應才是正確答案，所以將題目與3個選項一個一個仔細聽完並將錯誤選項逐步消除的「刪去法」，變得比以往更加有用了。

雖說只要善加運用「仔細聆聽的練習」加上「刪去法」就能攻略PART 2，但若使用改制前出版的舊版試題集，或是未掌握到最新出題傾向的試題集，那麼不管再怎麼練習，實際考試的時候還是賺不到分數的，這點得特別留意。

1 要懂得選擇「間接回應」！就母語者來說很自然的對話便是正確答案！

　　就母語者來說「很自然的對話」是怎樣的感覺呢？如果無法掌握這種感覺，就無法克服PART 2。

　　由於大學入學考等日本考試大多都是直接回應，所以若按照那種感覺答題，在PART 2就會陷入苦戰。目前的測驗中，答案是間接性的，而且稍微保有距離感的題目，25題之中會有15題左右，最好要先保有這樣的認知。

　　由於改制前出版的試題集中少有能巧妙納入這個部分的書，所以在挑選試題集時需多加留意。《TOEIC Listening & Reading官方全真試題指南》中也有收錄一些這類題目，所以可以挑來作，讓自己習慣這類題目。

　　官方全真試題在改制後出了好幾冊，不過據說要選間接回應選項的題目，還是出版日期較新的官方試題集收錄得較多。

　　就母語者來說「很自然的對話」是怎樣的感覺呢？我們就先藉由中文來掌握那種感覺吧。將問答的句子代換成中文，應該就能夠發現「啊～原來如此，對話確實是成立的呢」了。

藉由中文來習慣它吧！！

問題
ABC商店要怎麼去？

應答
那間店去年結束營業了。

問題
幾點會有前往DEF島的渡輪？

應答
冬天不開。

問題
你要買A牌的智慧型手機，
還是B牌的智慧型手機？

應答
我要多收集一些資料之後再決定。

問題
從車站到飯店的接送好像是免費的喔。

應答
這跟飯店官網寫的不太一樣耶……。

問題
哪裡可以找到這台機器的說明？

應答
我就很懂。

問題
為什麼我買的東西沒有送來？

應答
這已經不是我負責的了。

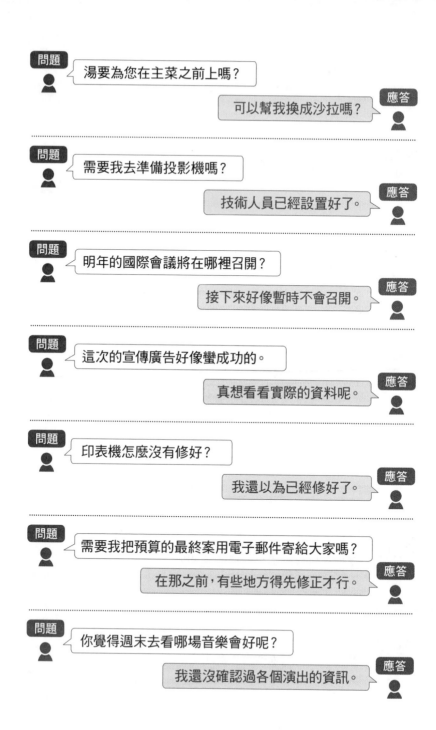

問題　湯要為您在主菜之前上嗎？

應答　可以幫我換成沙拉嗎？

問題　需要我去準備投影機嗎？

應答　技術人員已經設置好了。

問題　明年的國際會議將在哪裡召開？

應答　接下來好像暫時不會召開。

問題　這次的宣傳廣告好像蠻成功的。

應答　真想看看實際的資料呢。

問題　印表機怎麼沒有修好？

應答　我還以為已經修好了。

問題　需要我把預算的最終案用電子郵件寄給大家嗎？

應答　在那之前，有些地方得先修正才行。

問題　你覺得週末去看哪場音樂會好呢？

應答　我還沒確認過各個演出的資訊。

問題

你打算雇用誰來負責市場行銷？

應答

我現在還在想。

問題

這份文件上的數字有錯喔。

應答

都已經好幾個人確認過了……。

你弄懂「就母語者來說很自然的對話」是怎樣的感覺了嗎？

習慣這類應答的感覺是很重要的。

那麼，接下來就實際以英文來弄懂「就母語者來說很自然的對話」是怎樣的感覺吧。這裡會以問題→應答的順序呈現。

藉由英文來習慣它吧！！

問題

Could you let me know your availability?

應答

I emailed you my schedule this morning.

譯 可以讓我知道你什麼時候有空嗎？
我今天早上把我的行程用電子郵件傳給你了。

Haven't you finished the report yet?

The deadline was postponed.

譯 你還沒完成報告嗎？
截止日延後了。

How often do you travel to Europe on business?

I usually ask my assistant to go instead of me.

譯 你多久去歐洲出差一次？
我通常都會要求我的助理代替我去。

How long is the flight?

Let's look at the itinerary.

譯 飛行航程要多久？
我們來看看行程表。

When does the autumn session begin?

The schedule hasn't been decided yet.

譯 秋季班什麼時候開始？
時間表還沒有決定出來。

問題
Where did you save the documents for tomorrow's meeting?

應答
Stephan was the last one to work on it.

譯 你把明天會議的文件存在哪裡？
史蒂芬是最後一個使用的人。

問題
Which box should we use to ship these items?

應答
You had better ask Jenny.

譯 我們要使用哪一個箱子來運送這些貨品？
你最好去問珍妮。

問題
Where will the training session take place?

應答
It will be announced next week.

譯 訓練課程會在哪裡舉辦？
下週就會公布了。

問題
Which workshops are you planning on going to?

應答
Has the schedule already been posted?

譯 你打算去哪一些工作坊？
時間表已經張貼出來了嗎？

問題 **Isn't the electronics store offering a special discount this week?**

應答 **I think that was last weekend.**

譯 這間電器商店這禮拜不是有提供優惠折扣嗎？
我想那是上星期。

用人與人之間的對話來想想看吧。被用How often, Who, When, Where詢問時，不見得一定就會回答「頻率」、「人名」、「日程或時間」、「地點」。倒不如說，不這樣回答的時候還更多。就母語者來說很自然的對話，指的便是如此。

測驗改制後，在間接回應之中，正確答案為「較有距離感的回覆」的例子也變多了，所以題目和選項（不僅限於正確選項，錯誤選項也是）都必須仔細聆聽，這點相當重要。

為此，要用英文的狀態來理解英文，若都先一一翻成中文會耽誤到時間，因而漏聽下一個選項。最有效的方法，是看著官方全真試題等PART 2的錄音內容（英文），邊聽附錄CD，仔細確認自己哪個音沒有聽到、哪個模式的連音（音與音的接續）不容易聽取等問題，並且一直重聽這些自己不擅長的部分。

PART 2常出的間接且較有距離感的會話中，從簡單的題目到很難的題目都有，出題的幅度很廣。接下來，我將把間接程度分成0～7，並具體舉例說明。

間接程度0，指的是在5～6年之前都還經常當成正確答案的

「直接回應」，現在前半部分也會有4～5題會出這種題目。

與此相對，間接程度7則是指「間接並且非常有距離感的回覆」。

間接程度 **0**

問題 Where is the nearest post office?

應答 It's right across the street.

中譯 最近的郵局在哪裡？
就在對街。

問題 When will we be able to discuss the issue?

應答 We will meet next Monday.

中譯 我們什麼時候可以討論這個議題？
我們下週一會見面。

間接程度 **3**

問題 Where can I register for today's workshop?

應答 Please check the guide at reception.

中譯 我可以去哪裡報名今天的工作坊？
請至櫃台查詢指南。

間接程度 5

問題 Where is the lost and found desk?

應答 Actually, we don't have one.

中譯 失物招領的櫃台在哪裡？
其實，我們沒有這個櫃台。

間接程度 7

問題 Where's the telephone directory of attendees for the next conference?

應答 The list is only available to authorized personnel.

中譯 下一場會議與會者的電話錄在哪裡？
清單只有授權人士才能取得。

到了間接程度7，即便是擅長聽力的人，如果不熟悉TOEIC的話可能也選不出正確答案。最近間接程度5～7的題目增多，有時甚至會佔到10題以上。這種題目只能將選項全部聽完再判斷哪個最適當，投機的小手段在此是行不通的。

練習仔細聽英文比什麼都要重要，不過還是有些攻略的小訣竅，以下便列出作答時的重點供各位參考。

新制多益
出題重點

- 別選內含同樣發音或發音相似單字的選項

- 5W1H開頭的問句,應答時別選Yes/No開頭的選項

- 5W1H開頭的問句,務必聽取疑問詞、主詞、動詞

- 就算是一般的疑問句,也不一定總是用Yes/No回答

- 「附加疑問句」和「否定疑問句」可用一般疑問句相同的方式思考

- 要求選擇A或B的疑問句,可用以下4種模式回答

  1. 從A和B中選擇其一

  2. 回答「兩個都可以」

  3. 回答「兩個都不行」

  4. 就母語者來說很自然的對話

- 表達邀請或提議的疑問句,也是用母語者角度來作答

攻略技巧

2 選項中若有同樣發音或發音相似的單字 多半就是錯誤選項！

「選項帶有相同單字或發音相似的單字就別選」這招在PART 2效果超群。這是因為在PART 2的25題中，雖有3題左右正確答案是帶有相同單字或發音相似的單字的選項，但大多數情況下那些選項都是錯的（陷阱）。

這招很單純，所以在座位很差不容易聽清楚播放的聲音時，或是累了注意力無法集中時，還有因注意力中斷而有一瞬間漏聽時，都能夠使用。以下就透過例題向大家具體說明。

不要選擇相同的發音單字選項

Are you **familiar** with the new software **application**?

(A) Over 20 people have **applied**.
(B) Both employees and their **families** can join.
(C) I've just finished the training program.

> 帶有相同音節的單字！這就是陷阱！

中譯

你熟悉這個新軟體的應用嗎？

(A) 已經超過二十個人申請了。

(B) 員工和他們的眷屬都可以參加。

(C) 我剛結束訓練課程。

解析

(A)用了題目中使用過的單字的其他詞性applied，(B)也同樣用了families，然後再聽聽剩下的(C)，由於對話是成立的，所以(C)就是正確答案。

在本題中，3個選項裡有2個可用「使用帶有相同音節的單字」這個理由刪去。當然，在正式考試時也可能會遇到3個選項中只能刪去1個，或是3個選項內都未使用音節相同、發音相似的單字的題目，不過只要能從3個之中刪去1個，變成2選1，選中正確答案的機率就會上升許多。

刪去帶有相似發音的單字的選項！

Here's your copy of the accounting file.

(A) Yes, I did that already.

(B) Thanks, I was looking for that.

(C) You can place the coffee on my desk. ◄ 發音很像！這就是陷阱！

這是你會計資料的影本。

(A) 是的，我剛剛已經做過了。

(B) 謝謝，我正在找它。

(C) 你可以把咖啡放在我的桌上。

解析

　　(C)裡面有與題目使用的單字copy發音相似的coffee，對不擅長聽力的人來說，copy和coffee聽起來是一樣的，因此會覺得「啊，有聽起來跟題目用的單字一樣的單字，這個就是正確答案！」而選錯。

　　在本題中，和題目成立對話的(B)才是正確答案。

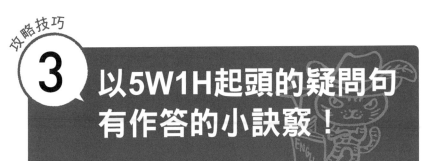

攻略技巧

3 以5W1H起頭的疑問句有作答的小訣竅！

Yes/No開頭的選項不要選！

針對5W1H開頭的疑問句，Yes/No起頭的應答句是錯誤答案，請不要選它。

以下就運用例題來具體說明。

What will happen if there aren't enough participants?
(A) No, but you can if you want.
(B) Only the ones in the drawer.
(C) The event might be rescheduled.

針對疑問詞開頭的問句，不能用Yes或No來回答。因此，(A)是錯誤答案。剩下就是(B)或(C)會是正確答案，但(B)作為回應很明顯偏題了，所以正確答案是(C)。

如果參與人數不夠的話，會發生什麼事？
(A) 不，但你想要的話，你可以這麼做。
(B) 只有在抽屜裡的那些。
(C) 會議可能會重新改期。

疑問詞、主詞和動詞務必要聽！

反覆練習讓自己能夠聽取全文是最為理想的。

Part 2的題目有35～45%是以5W1H疑問詞（具體來說是 where、when、what、which、who、how）開頭的疑問句。不過，只聽到疑問詞就能應付過去的僅有前半的4～5題而已。2016年5月TOEIC測驗改制以後，得聽完全文，並選擇「間接且對非母語者來說可能會感覺有些距離感，但對母語者來說對話是成立的」選項才行。

這裡就運用例題來具體說明。

問題 **Where did you buy these flowers from?**

應答 **Sarah bought them.**

中譯 你是在哪裡買到這些花的？
是莎拉買的。

　　在以前的測驗中，如果疑問句是以Where起頭，就只需要聽針對地點應答的選項就好，但現在的測驗中，選項卻必須一個一個仔細聽。在本題中，正確答案是由人名開頭的句子，針對「是在哪裡買的？」這個疑問，回答「是莎拉買的」。在這個回覆中，可以汲取到「我不知道是在哪裡買的」這個含意。

問題　**When do you expect the shipment to arrive?**

應答　**It is hard to say with this weather.**

中譯　你期望貨運什麼時候抵達？
　　　　這種天氣很難説。

　　對於When開頭的疑問句，並未以時間、日期或星期幾來回答，而是委婉暗示「（視天候而定所以）我不曉得」。

問題　**How do you commute to the office each day?**

應答　**I usually work from home these days.**

中譯　你每天都是怎麼通勤去上班的？
　　　　我這陣子都是在家工作。

　　因為是以How開頭詢問通勤方式的疑問句，所以會讓人不禁期待答案會是「搭捷運通勤」或是「開車通勤」等回覆。但是，回答「最近我都在家上班」也能接上對話。

　　最後，我們再來看1題以5W1H起頭的疑問句題目。請試著看出包含錯誤選項在內，題目是怎麼設下陷阱的。

Where can I get a refund on these items?
(A) Sure, if you have a receipt.
(B) I'd be happy to help you.
(C) That would be 44 dollars and 98 cents.

　　這是句以Where開頭的疑問句。對於「在哪裡退費？」這個問題，答案並非表示地點的直接回應，「我來為您處理」這種間接回應的(B)才是正確答案。這種對非母語者來說會覺得好像沒有正面回應，但對母語者來說對話是成立的選項，請學會將其正確選出。為了誤導只聽到題目中的refund（退費）的人，(A)用了receipt（收據），(C)則是出示了具體的金額，但兩者都無法用來答覆Where。

中譯

我可以去哪裡進行這些商品的退費？
(A) 當然，如果你有發票的話。
(B) 我很樂意幫助您。
(C) 這樣總共是 44 元又 98 分錢。

攻略技巧

4 不以5W1H起頭的
疑問句可不見得用
YES/NO就能回答

　　這邊我們就來攻略Do/Did you ......?、Are/Were you ......?、
Have you ......?或Should we ......?等不含疑問詞的一般問句題吧。

　　若是在大學升學考試之類的日本考試，回答這類疑問句時，大
多會用Yes/No起頭，但在TOEIC，正確答案可就不見得是用Yes/
No回答的選項了。有些時候以Yes/No回答的選項是正確答案，有
的時候不是。

　　那麼，選擇答案時的重點是什麼呢？就是選取「就母語者來説
很自然的對話」。該回應對於題目的問句來說，對話是否有自然地
延續下去，以這點來判斷出正確答案。

　　舉例來說，像是對於Did you decide to buy a new house?（你
決定要買新房子了嗎？）這個提問，回答I haven't saved enough
money yet.（我錢還沒存夠。）這樣。雖然沒用Yes/No，但對話是
成立的。

　　那麼，再來做做看下一個例題。

Did you review the documents for the client meeting?
(A) No, we can't.
(B) There was a misunderstanding.
(C) That is Jason's responsibility.

這是以Did開頭的疑問句。(A)的開頭雖然是No，但後面句子的意思與題目合不起來。(C)雖然沒有Yes或No，但卻很自然地接續了題目的對話。

題目不以5W1H的疑問詞起頭的情形，回答時有沒有Yes或No都無所謂，只要對話能自然延續就是正確答案。

中譯

你有先看過客戶會議的文件了嗎？
(A) 不，我們不能。
(B) 這之間有誤會。
(C) 那是傑森的責任。

再來1題吧。

🎧 21 | 🇨🇦 🇺🇸

Is the training session held in September every year?
(A) In seminar room 5.
(B) That's when new staff starts to work.
(C) Yes, if you have time.

這是以Is開頭的疑問句。對於「訓練課程都是每年九月舉行的嗎？」這個問題，回答「那是新員工開始工作的時候。」是很自然的，對話也有對應在一起。請抱持仔細聽完所有選項的心態來作答。

中譯

訓練課程都是每年九月舉行的嗎？
(A) 在第五會議室。
(B) 那是新員工開始工作的時候。
(C) 是的，如果你有時間的話。

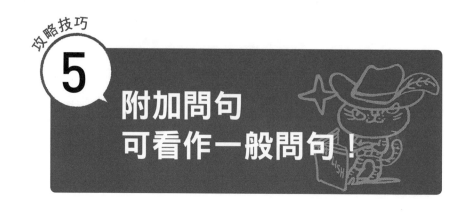

5

附加問句
可看作一般問句！

所謂的附加問句，是指像「～對吧？」這樣，向對方確認或尋求認同時使用的表達方式，若為肯定句就會在最後加上否定的問句，若為否定句則會在最後加上肯定的問句。

It's a beautiful day, isn't it?（今天是個美好的一天，不是嗎？）
肯定句 　　　　　　　↑逗號後面是「否定問句」

He isn't coming, is he?（他沒有要來，對吧？）
否定句 　　　　　　　↑逗號後面是「肯定問句」

附加問句每次會出1～2題，似乎不少人對它感到棘手。

不過，它其實不難。不用太在意它是附加問句這件事，用和一般問句同樣的解法來看它吧。正確答案不見得會是以Yes或No回答的選項這點，和一般問句是一樣的。

那麼，要說到選擇答案時的重點為何，那便是前面一再重複的「就母語者來說很自然的對話」。不管是Yes/No開頭的選項，還

是沒有Yes/No的選項，兩者皆可能是答案。因此有沒有Yes/No，在選擇正確答案時並不重要。

請試著作作看以下例題。

> You completed the Allenford project on schedule, didn't you?
> (A) The budget was finally approved.
> (B) The schedule seems to be acceptable.
> (C) Yes, but it required a lot of overtime.

與一般疑問句相同，需思考哪個選項才能接續對話。Yes或No有沒有都沒差，但(C)的話先說「對（按預定結束了）」，再接著回答「但是它需要大量加班」，所以可感受到對話自然地延續。此外，(B)用了題目中出現的單字schedule，試圖誤導考生。

中譯

你如期完成了 Allenford 的企畫，對吧？
(A) 預算終於通過了。
(B) 時程表看起來可以接受。
(C) 是的，但是它需要大量加班。

再來1題附加問句的例題吧。

Ms. Wilson is away on business this week, isn't she?

(A) It is right next to the bank.

(B) She should have asked first.

(C) I think I saw her this morning.

與一般疑問句相同,需思考哪個選項才能接續對話。被問到「威爾森小姐這週出差,是嗎?」,若選擇(C)「我想我今早有看到她」(暗指不是),對話便能成立。

中譯

威爾森小姐這週出差,是嗎?

(A) 它就在銀行旁邊。

(B) 她應該要先問的。

(C) 我想我今早有看到她。

攻略技巧 6

選擇問題 用4個模式就能作答！

　　所謂的選擇問題，是指「你要A or（還是）B呢？」「A比較好 or（還是）B比較好呢？」這種類型的問題。這類題目每次會出2題左右，答案的模式主要分為以下4種。

(1) 從A或B中選擇其一作為答覆

(2) 回答「哪個都行」，例如 "Either (one) is fine with me"

(3) 回答「兩個都不要（不好）」

(4) 就母語者來說很自然的對話

　　(2)這種類型雖然不常出，卻會在你忘記它的時候出現。選擇問題的題目大多很長，所以如果是(3)和(4)這種類型，就得確實聽取題目及選項的內容才有辦法作答。此外，即使是(1)，正確選項也幾乎都會將題目使用過的單字或說法換句話說，所以必須確實聽取選項，包括錯誤選項在內。因為如此，這對不善長聽力的人來說是蠻困難的題目。

　　另外，在作選擇問題時，請不要選Yes/No開頭的句子。

PART 1　照片描述

PART 2　應答問題

PART 3　簡短對話

PART 4　簡短獨白

TOEIC聽力測驗 預想模擬試題

雖然偶爾也會有Yes/No開頭的句子正確答案的情況，但絕大多數都是錯的。

　　那麼，我們就來做做看下面的例題吧。

Did she visit the clients last month, or was that in September?
(A) It's not that far from the highway.
(B) There are three flights daily.
(C) I don't think she has met them recently.

　　題目問到「A還是B」，正確答案(C)是將兩方皆予否定。當被問到「A還是B」的時候，並不一定非得選A或B不可。

　　在作這類題目時，特別需要將題目和各個選項仔細聽完。

中譯

她上個月有去拜訪客戶嗎？還是是在九月？
(A) 它沒有離高速公路那麼遠。
(B) 每天總共有三趟航班。
(C) 我不認為她最近有與他們會面。

　　我們再來看1題。

Do you want the green tea or the herbal blend?
(A) It is from China.
(B) Let me have a look at the menu again.
(C) Only on weekdays.

　　題目問及「A還是B」，(B)的回答不是選擇其一，而是採取「讓我再看菜單一次」這種其他形式的回應。儘管題目與此選項之間讓人感受到些許距離感，但對話是成立的。

　　像這樣帶有距離感的題目，3個選項都得好好聽完，再從3個之中選出（儘管間接但）較適切的選項。

中譯

你想要綠茶還是花草茶？
(A) 這來自中國。
(B) 讓我再看一次菜單。
(C) 只有在平日。

 **重要！注意！**

　　「你要A or（還是）B呢？」「A比較好or（還是）B比較好呢？」這類選擇問題中，若要從中選擇其一回答，有時候正確答案也可能會是沒有將A和B代換成別的詞彙，直接使用和題目相同單字的選項。

下面我們就透過例題來實際看看吧。

Would you like to use a credit card or pay cash?
(A) I may as well pay cash.
(B) Yes, that would be fine.
(C) I'll take both of them.

　　對於「你想要刷卡還是付現？」這個問題，正確答案是回答「付現」的(A)。遇到像本題的pay cash這種不容易換句話說的情況時，正確選項就有可能會使用和題目相同的單字。

中譯

你想要刷卡還是付現？
(A) 我不妨付現。
(B) 是的，那樣可以。
(C) 我兩個都要。

攻略技巧 7

邀請、提議問題
也是以對話自然展開
的感覺最為重要！

　　邀請、提議問題是指「你就（做）～如何？」「要不要（做）～呀？」這類問題。

例如，

Why don't you/we ------- ?
How about ------- ?
What about ------- ?
Would you like to ------- ?
Let's ------- .

等等，有各式各樣的講法。

　　出題數每次幾乎都是1～2題左右，其中又以「Why don't you ...?」開頭的題目最常出。

　　邀請、提議問題中，要選出正確答案最重要的一點，果然還是「選擇就母語者來說很自然的對話」。雖然偶爾也會出正確答案是「標準回應」、較為簡單的題目，不過頻率變低了。

偶爾會是正確答案的「標準回應」

● That's a good/great idea.
● Yes, I'd love to ------- .
● Sure, ------- .

Why don't you ......?是表示「你就（做）～如何？」這種意思的邀請、提議説法，和疑問詞Why開頭的疑問句完全是兩回事。疑問詞Why（為什麼）起頭的題目中，有Yes/No的選項是錯誤答案，但是在Why don't you ......?（你就（做）～如何？）這種表示邀請、提議的講法中，以Yes/No來回答也沒有任何問題。

題目常設有陷阱，對於Why don't you ......?開頭的題目，以Yes/No開頭的選項回答才是正確答案的這種案例偶爾會出現。

因此，請別把表示邀請、提議的Why don't you ......?和疑問詞Why弄混了。

那麼，就來作作看下面的例題吧。

Why don't you meet at the same time next week?
    (A) That's not on the agenda.
    (B) The conditions have changed.
    (C) Okay. That sounds good.

　　針對「要不要（做）～呢？」這種提議，正確答案(C)回答
「聽起來不錯」，是很簡單的標準回應。

中譯

你們何不下週同一時間見面？
(A) 這不在議程上。
(B) 情況改變了。
(C) 好的。聽起來不錯。

　　再來1題吧。

Why don't we go to a museum this weekend?
(A) It was established about 90 years ago.
(B) No, I don't think the material is weakened.
(C) Which one did you have in mind?

　　對於「這週末要不要一起去博物館？」這種提議，(C)回答
「你想好要去哪間博物館了嗎？」，而不是「好」或「不要」之類
直接的回應。正確答案就是這個雖然有些距離感但對話有成立的
(C)。最近這類型的題目增加了，所以請別被關鍵字拉走，要好好
聽取選項的內容。另外，選項(B)中用了與題目裡的weekend發音
相似的weakened，企圖誤導考生。

我們這週末何不去博物館？

(A) 它建造於約 90 年前。

(B) 不，我不認為材質有消弱。

(C) 你想好要去哪間博物館了嗎？

攻略技巧

8 以直述句回答直述句的題目攻略法

　　PART 2中段以後，會出現「以直述句回應題目的直述句」這種類型的題目。在這類題目中，「選擇就母語者來說很自然的對話」這點會變得更加重要。

　　那麼，就一起來看看下面這個例題吧。

I'm here to check in under the name "Ron Tyler."

(A) My assistant will check it for you.

(B) I'll take it.

(C) Could you spell that, please?

　　這是在飯店的櫃檯很常遇見的情形。「我是來辦理入住的」→(C)「能告訴我您的名字怎麼拼嗎？」這樣的對話有成立且接續得很自然。此外，選項(A)之中使用了題目裡有出現的單字check，企圖混淆視聽。

中譯

我來辦理入住，名字是「Ron Tyler」。

(A) 我的助理會替你確認。

(B) 我要買這個。

(C) 能告訴我您的名字怎麼拼嗎？

再來看1題吧。

You're offering this property at a very high price.
(A) Yes, we offer both brown and white rice.
(B) We could negotiate it.
(C) We're happy you enjoyed your stay.

在以直述句回應直述句的題目中，選擇正確答案的關鍵就只有確認對話是否有成立而已。當對方說「你這間房子賣得非常貴。」時，回答(B)「我們可以再談談」，對話就能夠成立。

選項有一部分沒聽清楚的時候，就請善用刪去法吧。另外，選項(A)用了和題目中出現的price發音相似的單字rice，企圖誘導考生。

中譯

你這間房子賣得非常貴。
(A) 是的，我們提供糙米和白米。
(B) 我們可以再談談。
(C) 我們很開心您住宿愉快。

攻略技巧

9 請託問題要先記住回答的方式！

　　表示請託的問題幾乎每次都會出，這類型題目出題時會使用以下這些說法。

● Could you ------- ?
● Can you ------- ?
● Would you ------- ?
● Would you mind --- ing?

　　想選出正確答案時，可參考以下說法。

答應請託的情形

● Sure, ------- .
● Right away.
● I'd love to ------- .
● Certainly, ------- .

帶有以上說法的句子。

拒絕請託的情形

● Sorry, ------- .
● Actually ------- .

- I'm afraid ------- .
- Unfortunately, ------- .

帶有以上說法的句子。

有沒有掌握住「選擇就母語者來說很自然的對話」的感覺，在這也同樣很重要。

比如說，題目「你能幫忙我找房子嗎？」→回答「你要找哪一區的？」這樣會話就有成立，所以是正確答案。

那麼，就來看看下面的例題吧。

Can you help me carry these boxes to the storage room?
(A) I'll do it as soon as I finish this email.
(B) They don't seem to mind.
(C) It is in meeting room number 3.

受託某件事情時，不立刻進行那件事而是給予「～結束之後再去做」這種回覆的題目相當常見。因此，正確答案是(A)。

中譯

你可以幫我把這些箱子搬進儲存室嗎？
(A) 我結束這封電子郵件後就去做。
(B) 他們感覺不在意。
(C) 在三號會議室。

接著再來看1題吧。

Can you recommend a dry cleaner in the area?
(A) The weather has been quite dry.
(B) All of my clothes are machine washable.
(C) Yes, it does look much cleaner.

　　這題是當對方拜託說「你可以推薦我這個地區的乾洗店嗎？」時，回答「我的衣服都是用洗衣機就能洗的」，暗示自己「不知道哪裡有洗衣店」。因此，正確答案是(C)。雖然這段對話很有距離感，但是成立的。「暗示對方察覺真意」在選擇間接回應時是非常重要的關鍵。另外，選項(A)和(C)中各自出現了題目中的單字dry和cleaner，企圖混淆考生。

中譯

你可以推薦我這個地區的乾洗店嗎？
(A) 最近天氣相當乾燥。
(B) 我的衣服都是用洗衣機就能洗的
(C) 是的，它看起來真的乾淨很多。

攻略技巧 10

讓你的否定疑問句登峰造極吧！

所謂的否定問句，是指利用否定式來提問的疑問句，例如以 Isn't he ......?取代Is he ......?，或以Aren't you ......?來取代Are you ......?。這在英文會話中用得很頻繁，所以TOEIC測驗也每次都會出好幾題。

美國人和加拿大人說話時，Isn't或Aren't的「t」的發音較輕，所以聽力較弱的人可能會沒聽到「t」的音，不小心聽成Is he ......?或Are you ......?。不過別擔心，因為不管是Is he ......?還是Isn't he ......?、Are you ......?還是Aren't you ......?，回答的方式都是一樣的。

比如說，不管對方是問Are you a student?，還是Aren't you a student?，只要是學生就回答Yes，不是學生就回答No。當然，這也和一般疑問句一樣，就算答覆中沒有Yes或No也可能是正確答案。

那麼，我們就來看看下面的例題。

Aren't you going to be transferred to the London branch from next month?
(A) I learned a lot there.
(B) No, it won't be until next year.
(C) I transferred at Victoria Station.

不管有沒有聽到句首Aren't的「t」，答覆都是一樣的，所以只要用和Are you going to ......?（一般疑問句）同樣的方式去思考就行了。不管句子裡有沒有Yes或No，只要選出雖然不是直接的回應但對話是成立的選項即可，所以可得知正確答案是(B)。

想要學會選出帶有距離感的解答，總之就是得去習慣它。另外，選項(C)中用了題目中有出現的單字transferred，企圖誤導考生。

中譯

你不是下週就要調去倫敦的分部了嗎？
(A) 我在那裡學了很多。
(B) 不，要到明年。
(C) 我在維多利亞站轉車。

\ 堅持到最後一刻！/

聽力部分常出現的英文單字

🎧 34

僅整理出最常出現的單字

PART 2

名詞

☐ assignment	任務、功課
☐ board (=board of directors)	董事會
☐ budget	預算
☐ figure	數據、數字
☐ hallway	走廊
☐ inventory	庫存
☐ invoice	費用清單
☐ laboratory	實驗室
☐ photocopier	影印機
☐ responsibility	責任
☐ shipment	運輸、貨運
☐ supplier	供應商
☐ supplies	（複數）供應（量、品）

動詞＆表示動作的說法

☐ apply for~	申請～
☐ approve	同意
☐ be delayed	延期
☐ be in charge of~	負責～
☐ be responsible for~	對～負責
☐ be supposed to do	應該要
☐ commute	通勤
☐ deliver	配送
☐ depend on~	依賴～；取決於～

☐ distribute	發放、分配	
☐ due	到期	
☐ expire	過期	
☐ extend	延長	
☐ had better do	最好做～	
☐ post	張貼	
☐ prefer	偏好	
☐ purchase	購買	
☐ review	再檢查、複審	
☐ set up~	設置、準備	

表示狀態的說法

☐ available	有空的	
☐ out of order	故障的	
☐ right away	立即	

PART 3

簡短對話

對話只會播放一次,聽完對話之後接著回答3題。試題本上僅印有題目、選項及圖表,沒有印對話內容。

PART 3 概要

題數 39題

作答時間 每題約8秒

題型範例 請先聽取對話，再從4個選項中選出答案。對話內容未印於試題本上，僅以錄音播放。

例

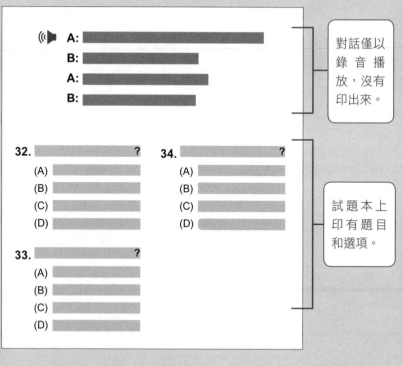

提前閱讀題目及選項是勝過一切的必勝法！

　　2016年5月TOEIC改制後，想用只靠作答技巧的學習方式來攻略PART 3變得困難許多。需要聽的句數增加，而且還新加入了「3人對話問題」、「圖表題」、「詢問意圖的題目」。要在PART 3大幅提升分數，提前閱讀題目和選項是不可或缺的，所以聽力不用說，閱讀能力也比以往更為必要。

　　現在的對話內容不像改制前來回3～4句就結束，有的題目會有6句、7句、8句。那類題目中，每次的發言較短，且話題會一直轉換，必須一面理解對話的內容一面掌握對話的走向，因此對於聽不懂、看不懂的人來說變成一項非常困難的測驗。

　　在這種情況下，PART 3的題數還從30題增加到39題，所以PART 3的重要性是日漸增加。另外，PART 3和PART 4的攻略法很像，所以若無法攻略PART 3就無法期望聽力部分的分數能大幅提升。

得預先閱讀題目 及選項！

PART 3中，預先閱讀印在試題本上的題目和選項，在知道會問什麼之後再聽對話，這點相當重要。

預先閱讀的作法

請按照以下步驟練習，讓自己能保持節奏持續到最後。

1　趁著播放PART 3說明時，預先閱讀第1大題32～34的題目及選項。

2　邊聽對話圈選答案。

3　趁播放32～34的題目時，預先閱讀下1題35～37的題目及選項。

這個預先閱讀的節奏若能維持到PART 3最後，也就是撐過13大題39小題不要亂掉，光只是這樣分數就能提升許多。

Part3
Directions:

《》錄音播放流程

32.
(A)
(B)
(C)
(D)

預先閱讀 32～34的 題目及選 項

1 趁在播放說 明的時候

33.
(A)
(B)
(C)
(D)

34.
(A)
(B)
(C)
(D)

圈選答案

(A)(B)(C)(D)

2 趁在播放對 話的時候

3 趁在播放32 ～34題目的 時候

35.
(A)
(B)
(C)
(D)

預先閱讀 35～37的 題目及選 項

36.
(A)
(B)
(C)
(D)

趁在播放35 ～37對話的 時候

37.
(A)
(B)
(C)
(D)

圈選答案

(A)(B)(C)(D)

重複 這個流程

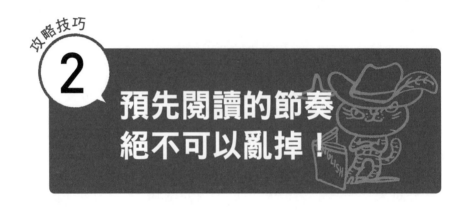

預先閱讀的節奏 絕不可以亂掉！

　　想要完美預讀題目及選項，就連對總能考取高分的人來說也不容易。如果預先閱讀的節奏亂掉了，就捨棄1小題（就是隨便選個答案）往前推進，或是放棄預讀選項只預讀題目之類的，總之就是得留意別打亂預讀的節奏。

　　沒辦法預讀全部題目和選項的人，最初可以先從只看題目，可以的話就看題目和4個選項中的2個選項，或是閱讀題目然後選項只看名詞、只看動詞等等開始習慣起。

　　如果只能先看題目，播放對話時就得將精神集中在「閱讀」選項上，而讓聽的動作變得草率，結果就會無法好好建立起預讀的節奏。

　　想要好好做到預讀，其中一項訣竅是利用測驗改制後出版的每一冊官方全真試題，全新投入邊預讀邊聽的練習，這麼做可以讓你抓住預讀的節奏。

　　另外一項非做不可的事，就是強化自己的閱讀能力。在閱讀部分拿到300分以上的閱讀能力是最低的門檻。當然，光這樣還是不夠的，請訓練自己取得更高的閱讀能力。

對話是按照「男→女→男→女」或是「女→男→女→男」的順序播放，而PART 3中間過後的題目有時會是「男→女→男→女→男→女→男→女」或「女→男→女→男→女→男→女→男」，對話來回6句、7句、8句才結束。

男性	
女性	
男性	
女性	
⋮	

 攻略的基本原則

- 題目的主詞若是 "the woman"   答案的提示應該就在女性的發言之中   〈 請注意聽女性的發言！

- 題目的主詞若是 "the man"   答案的提示應該就在男性的發言之中   〈 請注意聽男性的發言！

● 題目的主詞是 "the woman"，提示卻在男性的發言裡

● 題目的主詞是 "the man"，提示卻在女性的發言裡

> 雖然有例外，但比例卻不高，所以抱著「遇到例外時答錯就算了」的心情，好好掌握住基本原則吧。

以下我就透過例題來具體說明。

試題本上印有題目及選項。

Questions 32 through 34 refer to the following conversation.

32. What did the man read online?

    (A) Some entertainment blogs

    (B) Some academic ideas

    (C) Some executive travel websites

    (D) Some senior employee surveys

> 題目的主詞為男性，因此答案的提示應該就在男性的發言之中

33. What does the man invite the woman to do?

    (A) Visit his business

    (B) Speak at a book signing

    (C) Review his theories

    (D) Apply to become a manager

34. What does the woman say that she will do later today?

    (A) Wait for a fee payment

    (B) Use a new office workspace

    (C) Check some equipment

    (D) Look over her availability

> 題目的主詞為女性，因此答案的提示應該就在女性的發言之中

以下為錄音播放的對話。

M: I really enjoyed listening to your talk this morning, professor. I had read your theories on management on your blog...but seeing you in person was much more informative.

第32題的提示

W: Thank you, I'm glad that a senior executive like yourself found it helpful.

M: I did, and in fact, I'm sure that my managers could likewise benefit from hearing you speak...for your normal fee, of course. Could I e-mail you to arrange a talk at our firm?

第33題的提示

W: Certainly. I'll check my schedule when I get back to my office later today, and ...I'm sure that we could set something up.

第34題的提示

對話內容中譯

32到34題題目與以下對話有關。

男： 教授，我非常喜歡您今天早上的演講。我先前有閱讀過你部落格上關於管理的理論⋯⋯但是親眼見到您真的得到更多收穫。

女： 謝謝，我很高興像你這樣一位資深行政人員認為演講很有幫助。

男： 我是這麼認為的，而且事實上，我確信我的經理們也會在您的演講中受益匪淺⋯⋯當然是以您的正常收費來算。我可以寄電子郵件給您，在我們公司安排演講嗎？

女： 當然。我今天晚點回去辦公事時會確認我的時程表，而且⋯⋯我很確定我們可以計畫一些事情出來。

32. 男子在網路上讀了什麼？

(A) 一些娛樂部落格

(B) 一些學術概念

(C) 一些旅遊網站

(D) 一些資深員工調查

---

33. 男子邀請女子做什麼？

(A) 參觀他的公司

(B) 在簽書會上演講

(C) 審閱他的理論

(D) 申請擔任經理

---

34. 女子說今天晚點她將會做什麼事？

(A) 等待付款

(B) 使用新辦公室

(C) 確認一些設備

(D) 確認她有空的時間

攻略技巧

4 答案多半會隨著對話的展開依序出現

偶爾也會有例外，但基本上答案多半會按順序出現。

對話最開始的地方會有第1小題的答案，中段會有第2小題的答案，最後會有第3小題的答案，大致就是這樣的感覺。

有時也會有答案不按順序出現的情形，但並不常見，所以那種題目就算捨棄也沒關係。

只要知道這個法則，即便最開始的地方沒聽到也不要放棄，從中段之後重新集中精神，抱著「就算只有拿下第2小題也好（只有拿下第3小題也好）」這種多答對一題是一題的心情，繼續努力。

可以的話請盡力在3小題中答對2小題。

攻略技巧

5 記住常出現的題目類型

PART 3中有一些常出的固定題目，若能事先把握住那些題目，作答時就會輕鬆許多。至於哪些題目經常會出，只要確認測驗改制後出版的每一冊《TOEIC Listening & Reading官方全真試題指南》就能得知。

 第1小題常出的題目

---

1. **What are the speakers discussing?**
   說話者在討論什麼？

2. **What is the conversation about?**
   對話是關於什麼？

3. **Where does this conversation take place?**
   對話在哪裡進行？

4. **Where are the speakers (the man/woman)?**
   說話者（男子／女子）在哪裡？

5. **Where do the speakers (the man/woman) work?**
   說話者（男子／女子）在哪裡工作？

6. **Who most likely are/is the speakers (the man/woman)?**
   說話者（男子／女子）最有可能是誰？

　　這些題目的答案的提示大多會出現複數次，所以漏聽一次也不要放棄，只要掌握到第2次、第3次的提示或是對話整體的走向就能答對。

⟩ 應用篇 ⟨

此外，這種第1小題的典型題目有時也會出在第2小題。不過，原則上是第1小題常出的題目，所以就當作「就只是那個應用篇出在第2小題而已」吧。就算出在第2小題，作答的方式也和出在第1小題時一樣，也就是説提示應該會出現好幾次。

　　另一方面，第2小題和第3小題的題目，答案的關鍵字多半只會出現一次。因此，如果覺得自己沒聽到第1小題最初的提示，就先選填第2小題和第3小題的答案，最後再選第1小題的答案。若是想按順序選填而一直等待提示，可能會漏聽第2小題或第3小題的答案，這點必須多加留意。

 第2小題常出的題目

1. What is the problem?

問題為何？

2. What is the man/woman concerned about?

男子／女子擔憂什麼事情？

和第1小題相比，比較缺乏統一性，不過詢問特定時間、日期、資訊的題目大多會放在第2小題或是第3小題。詢問這些資訊的題目，答案多半只會提及一次，要是漏聽那個地方就無法作答。

　　對這類型的題目來說，預先閱讀非常重要。只要能夠預先閱讀，聽對話時就能特別注意對應的地方。

　　PART 3常出的典型對話走向裡，中段會產生「問題」或「擔憂事項」，後半的對話中則會將其解決，所以「問題為何？」「擔憂什麼事情？」這類題目多半出在第2小題。

應用篇

這種典型的第2小題題目有時也會出在第1小題。（出在第1小題時）對話的走向上，在前半便判明問題或擔憂事項，而非到了中段才揭示。這些題目就算出在第1小題，原則上還是第2小題類型的題目，所以答案的關鍵字多半只會說1次，能不能預先閱讀題目便是答題的關鍵。

 第3小題常出的題目

　　第3小題有各式各樣的題目，不過也有一些像是**What does the man/woman offer?**（男子／女子提供什麼？）或是**What will the man/woman most likely do next?**（男子／女子接下來最有可能做什麼？）等經常出在第3小題的題目。這些題目的答案多半在對話的後半，也就是說——題目的主詞如果是the man，就在最後發言的男性的話中；題目的主詞如果是the woman，就在最後發

言的女性的話中。

另外，第3小題中帶有will的題目也經常登場，例如**What does the man/woman say he/she will do?**（男子／女子說他／她接下來要做什麼？）。由於**will**是未來式，所以答案多半會在對話的後半男性或女性敘述接下來要做的事情的地方。

不管怎樣，找出要注意聽的部分仔細去聽，這點相當重要。也就是說，透過預先閱讀，從題目中掌握關鍵字或重要的表達，找出該聽的地方。那樣的話就能在聽的時候區分強弱（「重要的地方」與「聽聽就好的地方」）。

 其他常出題目

《詢問提議內容的題目》
詢問提議內容的題目定期會出。
What does the man/woman <u>suggest</u>?
男子／女子提議了什麼？
What does the man/woman <u>recommend</u>?
男子／女子推薦了什麼？

遇到這種情況，用以下這些表示提議的說法起頭的發言就是正確答案。

Why don't you ------ ?
How about ------ ?
What about ------ ?
Let's ------ .

《詢問委託內容的題目》

詢問委託內容的題目也是定期會出。

What does the man/woman <u>ask</u>?

男子／女子詢問了什麼？

What does the man/woman <u>request</u>?

男子／女子要求了什麼？

遇到這種情況，用以下這些表示委託的說法起頭的選項就是正確答案。

Could you ------ ?

Can you ------ ?

攻略技巧

6

測驗改制後新登場！

圖表題的攻略法

趁播放PART 1的說明與例題時確認圖表！

附有圖表的題目（圖表題）是在TOEIC改制以後才新導入的題型，會出在PART3和PART4的最後2～3題。

如果PART3出了2題那PART4就是3題，PART3出了3題那PART4就是2題，據說多數時候是像這樣以PART3和PART4相加為5題的模式來構成。

• 巧妙運用TOEIC測驗剛開始的時間

TOEIC是從早上9點開始考，起初會先播放PART1的題目說明，接著再播放PART1的例題。請運用那段時間，簡單確認過試題本上印在PART3與PART4的圖表。

• 3個題目中，有1題是不看圖表就無法作答的題目──

就是以Look at the graphic.起頭的那題！

由於PART3和PART4的圖表題中各有1題是不看圖表就無法作答的題目，所以那一題的問題與選項也要先看，先大概抓到得注意圖表的哪個部分。

不看圖表就無法作答的題目，務必要確認選項。圖表中，未出現在選項內的項目就會在對話中提及，所以要注意聽取那個部分。

圖表題範例

1 翻開試題本，找到帶有圖表的題目並加以確認

↓

2 確認3個題目之中以Look at the graphic. 起頭的那題

例 **Look at the graphic. What project will be postponed?**
(A) Yeseln Paper Co.
(B) Tunisk Gears, Inc.
(C) Garbiano Displays
(D) Alanjis Textiles

3 未出現在選項內的項目會在對話中提及，要注意聽

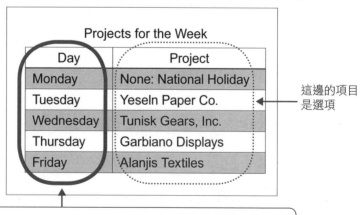

Projects for the Week

Day	Project
Monday	None: National Holiday
Tuesday	Yeseln Paper Co.
Wednesday	Tunisk Gears, Inc.
Thursday	Garbiano Displays
Friday	Alanjis Textiles

這邊的項目
是選項

這邊的項目應該會在對話中提及，要注意聽！
以本題來說，就是要注意聽星期。

65. **Why did the woman make the telephone call?**
(A) To ask about billing
(B) To discuss quality
(C) To make an assignment
(D) To confirm a shipment

66. **Look at the graphic. What project will be postponed?**
(A) Yeseln Paper Co.
(B) Tunisk Gears, Inc.
(C) Garbiano Displays
(D) Alanjis Textiles

這題就是不看圖表無法作答的題目。

67. **What will the woman most likely do next?**
(A) Wait for an e-mail
(B) Change the scope of a project
(C) Add members to a team
(D) Provide some contract details

以下是錄音播放的對話。

Questions 65 through 67 refer to the following conversation and chart.

W: Chad, I'd like your group to get out to the Zanalak Office Building on Wednesday. We've got a contract with a new client who wants photocopiers installed that day.

M: Uh...well, Ms. Gupta, I've already got another assignment...uhm...well, to be honest, the entire week's schedule is already full. I'm not sure if I could squeeze anything new in.

W: Then I'll clear your Wednesday schedule for you. I'll shift your projects of that day back another 10 days or so.

M: Ah...okay, then, I can do it. But ...uh...could you send me the project details? After I get an idea of the size and scope of the project, I can decide how many people I would need and who to bring with me.

W: OK, I'll be e-mailing those in an attachment to you within the next few hours.

⋯⋯⋯⋯⋯⋯⋯⋯⋯⋯⋯⋯⋯⋯⋯⋯⋯⋯⋯⋯⋯⋯⋯

題目、選項與圖表的中譯

當週企畫

星期	企畫
星期一	無：國定假日
星期二	Yeseln Paper 社
星期三	Tunisk Gears 社
星期四	Garbiono Displays 社
星期五	Alanjis Textiles 社

65. 為何女子要打這通電話？

(A) 詢問帳單

(B) 討論品質

(C) 進行指派

(D) 確認貨運

66. 請看圖表。哪一項企畫將會被延期？

(A) Yeseln Paper 社

(B) Tunisk Gears 社 ◄── 因為是星期三的企劃，所以這個是正確答案。

(C) Garbiono Displays 社

(D) Alanjis Textiles 社

67.女子接下來最有可能做什麼？

   (A) 等待電子郵件

   (B) 改變企劃的範疇

   (C) 加入新成員到團隊裡

   (D) 提供一些合約細節

⋯⋯⋯⋯⋯⋯⋯⋯⋯⋯⋯⋯⋯⋯⋯⋯⋯⋯⋯⋯⋯⋯⋯⋯⋯⋯⋯⋯⋯⋯⋯⋯⋯⋯⋯

對話內容中譯

65到67題題目與以下對話有關。

女：查德，我希望你的團隊星期三去薩那拉辦公大
樓。我們有了新客戶，對方希望那天可以安裝影
印機。

男：恩⋯⋯是這樣的，古波塔小姐，我已經有另外一
項任務了⋯⋯恩⋯⋯這樣的話，老實說，我整個
禮拜的行程都是滿的。我不確定我能否有辦法再
接其他新的工作。

女：那我就把你星期三的行程都清空。我會把你那天
的企劃往前移十天左右。

> 星期三是
> 關鍵詞

男：啊⋯⋯好的，那麼，我就可以做了。不過⋯⋯恩
⋯⋯你可以把企劃細節傳給我嗎？有了企劃大小
和規模的概念後，我就可以決定我需要帶多少人
跟我一起去。

女：好，我接下來幾個小時內會將細節作為附件，傳
電子郵件給你。

7

測驗改制後新登場！

3人對話的攻略

3人對話題型中，在播放對話之前，會先有**Questions xxx through xxx refer to the following conversation with three speakers**.（問題XXX到XXX請參照下面三人的對話）這樣的說明。只要有注意聽with three speakers的部分，就能事先掌握到「這是3人對話」。

• 3人對話題也要在預讀時注意題目的「主詞」

3人對話題出在前半時比出在後半時簡單，所以如果出在前半，請3題都要答對。3人對話題和2人對話題一樣，要先透過預先閱讀注意題目的主詞是男性還是女性再來聽對話，這點相當重要。3人對話的時候，會有2位男性與1位女性（男1、男2、女），或是1位男性與2位女性（男、女1、女2）。不少人無法區分同性2人的聲音，因而覺得很困難，但即使無法區分聲音，單只是藉由預讀掌握題目的主詞，知道說出答案的會是女性還是女性，就能讓你在作答時輕鬆很多了。

每個人的發言都很短，話題也會不停轉換，
所以必須確實掌握住對話整體的走向

遇到較難的題目，不必以全對為目標，
只要3小題中有2小題能確實答對即可

攻略技巧

8

測驗改制後新登場！

詢問意圖的題目在預先閱讀時只需閱讀 " " 內的文字即可

這是TOEIC測驗改制後才新導入的題目，PART 3和PART 4會各出2～3題。

詢問意圖的題目，指的是下列這類題目，對話部分會畫底線是其特徵。預先閱讀時只要看 " " 內的文字就夠了。

---

1. **What** does the man/woman **mean** when he/she says,

   "   "?

2. **What** does the man/woman **imply** when he/she says,

   "   "?

3. **Why** does the man/woman **say**,

   "   "?

   中譯

1. 男子／女子在說 "   " 時是什麼意思？

2. 男子／女子在說 "   " 時是暗示什麼意思？

3. 為什麼男子／女子要說 "   " ？

其實，這個「詢問意圖題」對TOEIC 900分以上的人來說也很困難，因為若無法從頭正確聽取到一定程度，或是" "部分的前後無法正確聽取到，就無法作答。

此外，題目中" "部分如果較長，通常選項也會較長，預先閱讀時會被占去許多時間。因此，詢問意圖題可能會大幅打亂預讀的節奏，使得後面的題目接連出錯。

只要被詢問意圖題絆住，之後就會陷入惡性循環，讓預讀的節奏變得亂糟糟。一旦變成這樣，PART 3攻略失敗也會影響到PART 4，乃至整個聽力部分的失敗都有可能。

TOEIC 600分以下的人，遇到詢問意圖題時可以隨便選一個選項，直接進到下一題。即便是對目標800分以上的人來說，做出只要能對一半就不錯了的判斷，跳過看起來很難的題目才是上策。

以下我們就透過例題，來看看詢問意圖題是怎樣的題目。

• 詢問意圖題範例

52. **What does the woman mean when she says, "Yes, I'm sorry to say that's the only option at this point"?**

(A) A mistake was made by the man.
(B) A firm's policy cannot be changed.
(C) A product is not covered by insurance.
(D) A regulation requires him to make a report.

只預先閱讀
" "內文字

以下是錄音播放的對話。

Questions 50 through 52 refer to the following conversation.

M: Hello, I'm calling about a package delivery notice placed on my door by your company. It states the package is still at your office. Could you deliver it again tomorrow morning?

W: We certainly can, but does the notice read "Signature required"?

M: It does. I suppose that means that the package has to be signed for upon delivery.

W: Yes, I'm sorry to say that's the only option at this point. So please ensure that you or someone else is home when it comes. It should arrive sometime before 11:00 A.M.

對話內容中譯

50到52題題目與以下對話有關。

男：嗨，我來電是想詢問貴公司放置在我門口的包裹寄送通知。它寫著包裹仍然在你們的辦公室。請問貴公司可以明天早上再寄送一次嗎？

女：我們當然可以，但是請問通知上有寫「需要簽名」嗎？

男：有。我想那代表包裹在送達時需要簽收。

女：是的，我很抱歉目前這是唯一的選擇。所以請確保包裹到達時您或是其他人是在家的。包裹應於早上十一點前送達。

題目、選項與圖表的中譯

52. 女子說「是的，我很抱歉目前這是唯一的選擇」時，是什麼意思？

(A) 男子犯了一個錯誤。

(B) 一間公司的政策是無法更改的。

(C) 產品沒有納入保險。

(D) 有一項規定需要他做一份報告。

攻略技巧

9

看見most likely或 probably、imply等 用字就能認出推測題

有些題目中會出現most likely（最有可能），偶爾也會有意思和most likely一樣的probably，但最常出現的還是most likely。

舉例來說，就是Where does the man most likely work?（男子最有可能在哪裡工作？），或是What will the woman most likely do next?（女子接下來最有可能做什麼？）這類題目，每次都會出好幾題。遇到帶有這些單字的題目時，對話中通常沒有直接導向答案的英文，多半需要自行推測才能作答。

不習慣TOEIC的人似乎就很容易出錯。帶有most likely或probably的題目主要出在第1小題和第3小題，尤其是第1小題特別常見。

另一方面，imply（暗示）在攻略技巧8之中說明過的「詢問意圖題」裡也會使用，這也是必須推測答案的題目。

我覺得對這種不會直接說出答案、需要自行推測的題目感到棘手的考生蠻多的。解題時請謹記要「推測」！

10 打電話的目的通常在開頭就會先說

　　電話中的對話也很常拿來出題。出現電話對談時，就有可能會出Why is the man/ woman calling?（男子／女子為什麼要來電？）或是What's the purpose of the call?（此通電話的目的是什麼？）這類詢問打電話目的的題目。工作方面的電話大多會在最初講明打電話的目的，因此答案多半會出現在前半，請意識著這點去聽前半部分。

　　此外，講述打電話的目的時，經常會用I am calling to...（我來電是要……）或I am calling because...（我打來是因為……）等開頭。只要出現這類說法，就要特別注意聽。

題目範例

Why is the woman calling?

女性的發言中會有提示！

要從女性的發言中

I am calling <u>to</u> inform you that the order form you submitted yesterday seems to be wrong.

得知打電話的目的，就要聽 to 以下的部分。

「我來電是要通知你，你昨天繳交的訂單格式似乎是錯的。」

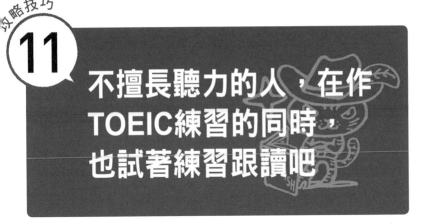

攻略技巧

11

不擅長聽力的人，在作 TOEIC練習的同時， 也試著練習跟讀吧

不擅長聽力的這種人，除了缺乏聽英文的經驗外，一般也缺乏單字量與對文法的理解。如果文法很弱，閱讀英文時很花時間，就無法順利預讀題目和選項。而且若是這些能力較弱，只要播放的對話一變成比較長的複句，就會無法理解意思。就如我前面也一直反覆提起的一樣，這雖然是聽力部分的測驗，但其實想要提升分數，閱讀能力也有很大的影響。

另一方面，努力苦讀入學考，對文法和單字有一定程度的理解，也看得懂一定程度的英文，但卻因為缺乏聽英文的經驗而聽不懂的人也大有人在。對於那樣的人，我建議要練習跟讀（或是疊讀★譯註）。

所謂的跟讀法（Shadowing），就是一邊聽英文一邊模仿發音的一種訓練法。和聽完整句英文後才重覆的「複誦法（Repeating）」不同，跟讀法是在聽到英文之後像影子一樣緊接著發音的練習。

★譯註：疊讀法（Overlapping），進行訓練的方式為播放與文字內容相同的英文語音，同時看著文字唸出上面的語句，唸出的語句需與播放的語音重疊。

除了進行提高PART 3分數的預讀練習外（還是以此為主），每天再加上30分鐘的跟讀訓練持續10天左右，光只是這樣聽力就會進步許多。

想提高ＴＯＥＩＣ分數，可以使用官方全真試題《TOEIC Listening & Reading官方全真試題指南》的題目當作素材。每天1大題，花30分鐘左右一直反覆跟讀同一篇題目就會有不錯的效果，用來練習的題目可以天天替換。

攻略技巧

12

答案卡上只要 先用點作個記號

　　PART 3的結果，取決於能夠集中多少在「預先預讀」和「聽取」上，若是一格一格仔細填畫答案卡，理所當然就會佔用到預讀和聽取的時間。用畫卡專用的鉛筆或自動筆在答案卡上先畫個點，之後再利用播放PART 3最後的第68～70題的題目的時間一口氣填滿所有格子，是較佳的做法。

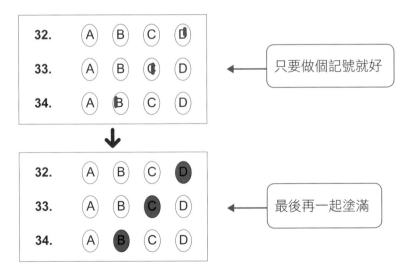

只要做個記號就好

最後再一起塗滿

\ 堅持到最後一刻！/

聽力部分常出現的英文單字

🎧 35

僅整理出最常出現的單字

PART 3&4

名詞

appliance	器具、設備
application	應用
assembly line	生產線
colleague	同事
complaint	抱怨
consumer	消費者
coworker	同事
deal	交易
destination	目的地
editor	編輯
electrician	電工
estimate	預估
exhibition	展覽
expense	花費
feature	特色、特徵
fund-raising	募資
ingredient	成份
issue	問題；發行；刊號
job opening	職缺
landscaping	造景
merger	合併
museum	博物館
prescription	處方籤
property	資產
quantity	數量
quote	引言
real estate	不動產
refreshment	點心
renovation	翻修、更新
resume	履歷表

126

☐	status	狀態、狀況
☐	strategy	策略
☐	subscription	訂閱
☐	transportation	運輸（方式）
☐	warehouse	倉庫

動詞＆表示動作的說法

☐	award	獎項
☐	be concerned about ~	擔憂～
☐	be eligible for ~	有資格～的
☐	confirm	確認
☐	expedite	迅速處理
☐	place an order	下訂單
☐	postpone	延期
☐	put together ~	把～放置在一起
☐	release	釋出；發表
☐	remind	提醒
☐	renew	更新
☐	replace	代替
☐	return a call	回電
☐	specialize in ~	專精於～
☐	submit	提交
☐	transfer	轉運
☐	upgrade	升級
☐	verify	核對

表示狀態的說法

☐	affordable	可負擔的
☐	complimentary	免費贈送的
☐	overnight	一整夜的
☐	promising	有前途的
☐	ready	準備好的
☐	temporary	暫時的
☐	upcoming	即將到來的

PART 4

簡短獨白

聽完電話語音留言、會議內容節錄、廣播（通知）等獨白後，接連回答3小題。試題本上僅印有題目、選項及圖表，未印有獨白。

PART 4 概要

題數 30題

作答時間 每題約8秒

題型範例 試題本上僅有印題目及選項。請先聽取獨白,再從4個選項中選出答案。獨白內容未印於試題本上,僅以錄音播放。

例

獨白僅以錄音播放,沒有印出來。

71. _____ ?
(A) _____
(B) _____
(C) _____
(D) _____

72. _____ ?
(A) _____
(B) _____
(C) _____
(D) _____

73. _____ ?
(A) _____
(B) _____
(C) _____
(D) _____

試題本上印有題目和選項。

運用PART 3的訣竅！
養成閱讀長篇文章的能力也是1種攻略法

　　PART 4原則上可用和PART 3一樣的方法攻略。和PART 3中一再重覆的一樣，一題一題確實預讀題目與選項這件事十分重要。

　　PART 4也在2016年5月測驗改制後加入了新題型。

　　新加入的題型是圖表題及詢問意圖題。

　　此外，改制後的測驗，播放的獨白變多變長了，而且PART 4和PART 3相比，每一句的長度有較長的傾向，所以我認為不具備閱讀英文長篇文章能力的人將會陷入苦戰，因為那種人的耳朵僅能捕捉到單字，而無法進一步理解句子的內容。另一方面，擅長閱讀長篇文章的人，由於PART 4的故事比PART 3更具一貫性，所以不少人會覺得很簡單。

　　因此，PART 4在掌握攻略法和練習聽力的同時，要進行閱讀1篇較長文章（有使用關係代名詞或分詞等修飾語且每句長度較長的文章）的訓練，需從頭開始並維持一定的速度閱讀，然後練習讓自己能快速讀懂TOEIC PART 7（閱讀理解）那樣較長的題目文章也很有效。

攻略技巧

1 得預先閱讀題目及選項！

　　請利用播放PART 4說明的時間，預先閱讀最初的1大題71～73的題目和選項。播放獨白時在答案卡上的正確選項點個點（只要先做個記號就好，之後再塗滿），然後趁播放71～73的題目時趕快先看下1大題74～76的題目和選項。照著這個節奏做完整個PART 4。

預先閱讀的作法

　　請按照以下步驟練習，讓自己能保持節奏持續到最後。

　①　趁著播放PART 4說明時，預先閱讀第1大題71～73的題目及選項。

　②　邊聽獨白邊圈選答案。

　③　趁播放71～73的題目時，預先閱讀下1大題74～76的題目及選項。

Part4
Directions:

((▶ 錄音播放流程

71.
- (A)
- (B)
- (C)
- (D)

預先閱讀 71～73的題目及選項

72.
- (A)
- (B)
- (C)
- (D)

73.
- (A)
- (B)
- (C)
- (D)

圈選答案

Ⓐ Ⓑ Ⓒ Ⓓ

74.
- (A)
- (B)
- (C)
- (D)

預先閱讀 74～76的題目及選項

75.
- (A)
- (B)
- (C)
- (D)

76.
- (A)
- (B)
- (C)
- (D)

圈選答案

Ⓐ Ⓑ Ⓒ Ⓓ

1 趁在播放說明的時候

2 趁在播放獨白的時候

3 趁在播放71～73題目的時候

趁在播放74～76對話的時候

重複這個流程

2

答案多半按獨白的
先後依序出現

　　和PART 3一樣，答案大多會按照獨白開始到結束的順序出現。也就是說，獨白開頭的部分會有第1小題的答案，中段會有第2小題的答案，後半則會有第3小題的答案。

　　不擅長聽力的人，就算無法掌握到對話的走向，剛開始抱著「至少前半會有答案的第1小題，和專注聽後半就會知道答案的第3小題絕對要答對！」這種心情，提醒自己要在3小題中拿下2小題，這也是一種方式。

攻略技巧

3

要留意題目的種類

和PART 3相同，看清楚題目的類型相當重要。

第1小題多半會提示好幾次，而且得聽懂一定長度的句子才有辦法作答，而第2小題和第3小題則大多只會提示一次。

就這個層面上來説，預先閱讀第2小題和第3小題的題目及選項變得更為重要。透過預讀找出需注意聽的關鍵字（關鍵字問題在第2小題特別會出），然後在聽取獨白的時候千萬別錯過它。

 第1小題常出的題目

---

1. What type of industry/company does the speaker work in?

2. What kind of business is the speaker most likely calling?

3. Who is the speaker most likely calling?

4. What kind of event is taking place?

5. Who most likely are the listeners?

6. Where does the speaker most likely work?

7. What is the report/broadcast mainly about?

---

1. 說話者在哪個產業／公司工作？
2. 說話者最有可能來電詢問何種事務？
3. 說話者最有可能打給誰？
4. 什麼活動正在進行中？
5. 聽者最有可能是誰？
6. 說話者最有可能在哪裡工作？
7. 報告／廣播主要和何事有關？

這些題目多半

① 答案的提示會出現數次

② 得聽取較長的句子

所以就算錯過了一次也請不要放棄。

應用篇

這種第1小題的典型題目有時也會出在第2小題。不過，原則上是第1小題常出的題目，所以就當作「就只是那個應用篇出在第2小題而已」吧。

就算出在第2小題，作答的方式也和出在第1小題時一樣，也就是說提示會出現好幾次，或是得聽取較長的句子才能作答。

第2小題和第3小題的提示通常只會出現1次，所以如果覺得自己沒聽到第1小題的提示，就先選填第2小題和第3小題的答案，再回頭選第1小題的答案。

　　這是因為若是想按順序點選而一直等待提示，可能會漏聽第2小題或第3小題的提示。由於第1小題的提示通常會出現好幾次，所以很多時候即便沒聽到獨白開頭的提示後來也能作答。

 第2小題常出的題目

　　第2小題會問具體的內容或特定的內容，且答案的提示多半只會出現1次。因此，在預先閱讀題目的時候，要先抓到得注意什麼部分再去聽獨白，只要能做到這點就能選出正確答案。

> **應用篇**
>
> 這種題目有時也會出在第1小題，但基本上是第2小題常出的題目，所以就當作「就只是那個應用篇出在第1小題而已」吧。就算出在第1小題，作答的方式也和提示只會出現1次的第2小題一樣。

 第3小題常出的題目

1. What are the listeners asked to do?
2. What does the speaker ask listeners to do?
3. What will the speaker most likely do next?
4. What does the speaker offer to do?

137

1. 聽眾被要求做何事？
2. 說話者要求聽者做何事？
3. 說話者接下來最有可能做何事？
4. 說話者願意主動做何事？

上面3和4這種題目在PART 3也經常出在第3小題。

除了上列這些以外，還有其他各式各樣的問題，但總之第3小題的答案大多會出現在獨白的後半，所以請認真去聽後半。

無論如何，只要能找出非聽到不可的部分，就能夠注意去聽它。也就是說，透過預先閱讀先抓住必須聽到的關鍵字或重要表達，確定該聽的部分，就能讓你在聽的時候區分強弱，知道哪些是「重要的地方」和哪些是「聽過就好的地方」。

和PART 3一樣，維持預讀的節奏非常重要。為此，不光是題目，最好也要能預讀選項。若是無法預讀選項，就得邊聽獨白邊從頭仔細閱讀選項，這麼一來焦點便偏向閱讀，而無法專注在聽力上面。此外，一旦焦點轉向閱讀，就難以順利建立預讀題目及選項的節奏。理想上，最好能預先閱讀題目及全部選項，但這需要高度的閱讀能力，所以就算只能看2個選項也好，請盡力讓自己能夠連選項也一起預讀。

至於如何訓練預讀，請利用整套《TOEIC Listening & Reading官方全真試題指南》不斷練習。PART 3、PART 4的分數會根據你練習的量而有明顯的差距。

攻略技巧

4

測驗改制後新登場！

圖表題的攻略法

　　這是在TOEIC改制以後才新導入的題型，會出在PART3和PART4的最後2～3題。如果PART3出了2題那PART4就是3題，PART3出了3題那PART4就是2題，多數時候是像這樣以PART3和PART4相加為5題的模式來構成。

　　圖表題在預讀題目及選項時有幾點必須注意。每大題中都會有1小題得看著圖表作答，所以在預讀時，不要只確認圖表是什麼內容，而需連該題的題目及選項也一併確認，讓自己對於需留意圖表的什麼地方有個底。

　　PART 4的圖表題攻略法與PART 3相同，只要徹底掌握住P.111～P.115的答題方法，這邊就能成為你的得分源。

詢問意圖的題目很難，可視目標分數捨棄

測驗改制後新登場！

  這是TOEIC測驗改制後才新導入的題目，PART 3和PART 4都會各出2～3題。

  詢問意圖的題目，指的是下列這類題目，對話部分會畫底線是其特徵。預先閱讀時只要看 " " 內就夠了。

1. **What** does the speaker **mean** when he/she says,
   "   "?

2. **What** does the speaker **imply** when he/she says,
   "   "?

3. **Why** does the speaker **say**,
   "   "?

中譯

1. 説話者説 "   " 時是什麼意思？

2. 説話者説 "   " 時， 暗示著什麼？

3. 為什麼説話者要説 "   " ？

和PART 3一樣,這種「詢問意圖題」很難,即便是對TOEIC 900分以上的人來說也相當棘手。因為不少題目若無法從頭正確聽取到一定程度,或是" "部分的前後無法正確聽取到,就無法作答。

此外,題目中" "部分如果較長,通常選項也會較長,預先閱讀時會被占去許多時間。這麼一來,預讀的節奏可能會被大幅打亂,使得後面比較簡單的題目也失分。

在PART 3也有提過,遇到詢問意圖題時隨便選一個選項,直接進到下一題也是種方法。

即便是對以取得高分為目標的人來說也一樣,與其打亂預讀的節奏,不如跳過看起來很難的題目。

攻略技巧 6
題目說明中也會有提示！

播放獨白之前，會先播放Question 71 through 73 refer to the following telephone message.（問題 71 到 73 請參照下面的電話留言）這類題目說明。只要聽到這裡就會知道「接下來是電話留言」。其他像是「廣播（＝通知）」、「演講」、「廣告」等，也可以透過題目說明掌握到接下來要播放的獨白類型。

題目根據獨白類型各有特徵，請利用整套《TOEIC Listening & Reading官方全真試題指南》，事先掌握住各種情境的題目特徵。

攻略技巧

7

語音留言
絕對會出好幾題！

電話的語音留言題一定會出好幾題。

只要有電話上的對話，就很容易出現像是Why is the speaker (the man/woman) calling?（為什麼說話者〔男性／女性〕要打電話來？）或是What's the purpose of the call?（這通電話的目的是什麼？），這類詢問打電話之目的的題目。由於打電話的目的大多會在最前面提及，所以答案的提示多半是在前半部，請注意聽前半部。

此外，提到打電話的目的時，經常會使用I am calling to ......（我來電是要……）、I am calling because ......（我打電話來是因為……）或是I am calling to let you know ......（我來電是要讓你知道……）開頭的句子，如果聽到這類講法，就要特別留意。

8

有些情境 是經常出現的！

PART4中有不少會重複拿來出題的「常見故事」，因此對付起來也比PART3要來得容易。視故事而定，題目也有不少是「常見」的。所以請努力作完每一冊《TOEIC Listening & Reading官方全真試題指南》，將常出現的故事以及每個故事容易出的題目記在腦海裡。

接下來就來依序為大家具體介紹常見的故事及常出的題目。

· ·

 telephone message（電話語音留言）

10題之中會有3題以上是語音留言。由於是PART4內出題數最多的題型，所以勢必得攻略它才行。

故事情節分為3種類型：①私人致電企業團體時遇到語音留言；②企業團體致電私人住家留下語音留言；③同一企業內各部門間的語音留言。其中最近越來越常出的是③這種類型。

新制多益
出題重點

常出的題目類型

- **Why is the speaker calling?**
  為什麼說話者要打電話來？

- **What's the purpose of the call?**
  此通來電的目的為何？

- **What type of business is the speaker most likely calling to talk about?**
  說話者來電最有可能談論的事情是什麼？

- **Where is the speaker calling from?**
  說話者是從什麼地方撥打電話？

- **Where (In which department) does the speaker most liky work?**
  說話者最有可能在哪裡（哪個部門）工作？

- **What kind of company does the speaker work for?**
  說話者任職於哪種型態的公司？

- **What does the speaker ask the listener to do?**
  說話者要求聽者做什麼事？

- **What problem does the speaker mention?**
  說話者提及了什麼問題？

- **What does the speaker offer to do?**
  說話者主動提出幫忙何事？

- **Whom is the message intended for?**
  此訊息應是傳達給何者？

- **Who is most likely the listener?**
  聽者最有可能為何人？

- **What does the speaker request?**
  說話者要求何事？

- **What does the speaker say he/ she will do?**
  說話者說他／她會做何事？

---

 excerpt from a meeting（會議的一部分）

每次多半會出1～2題，是PART4中出題數排名第二的題型。情節是從較長的會議中擷取出的一部分，會議內容五花八門，例如與開發新產品相關的事、與業績相關的事、與產品問卷相關的事等等。

常出的題目類型

- **What is the speaker mainly discussing?**
  講者主要在談論什麼？

- **What does the speaker say he/ she will do?**
  講者說他／她會做何事？

- **Who are most likely the listeners?**
  聽者最有可能為何人？

- **What problem does the speaker mention?**
  講者提及了什麼問題？

- **Where does the speaker/ listeners probably work?**
  講者／聽者（們）最有可能在哪裡工作？

- **What is the purpose of the meeting?**
  這場會議的目的為何？

- **What will the speaker provide next?**
  講者接下來會提供什麼？

- **What will happen on/ at _____?**
  在×××（日期／地點）會發生什麼事？

- **What type of information are the listeners asked to provide?**
  聽者（們）被要求提供什麼資訊？

 broadcast（廣播）

情境會有各種新聞、錄音室中請到來賓參與的節目、來自錄音室外的報導、廣告等等。若情境為有來賓參與的節目，題目就常會問來賓的職業和他最近做了什麼事情。

常出的題目類型

- **What is the purpose of the broadcast?**
  廣播的目的為何？

- **What is being announced?**
  何事正在進行公告？

- **What can listeners do at the company's website?**

在公司的網站上，聽者可以做什麼事？

- **Why should listeners visit a website?**
  為什麼聽者要去瀏覽網站？

- **What is （公司名、人名等）known for?**
  XXX 有名的地方是什麼？

- **What type of service is being discussed?（內容為廣告時）**
  正在討論何種服務？

- **What will happen on/at（日期、時間等）?**
  在 XXX 的時候會發生何事？

- **Who is the intended audience for the advertisement?**
  廣告的目標觀眾是誰？

- **What will be discussed after the commercial / weather forecast?**
  在廣告／氣象預報後會討論何事？

 announcement（公告、通知、宣告）

　　情境大多是各種活動的通知、研修或講座中廣播的開頭部分、社內廣播、機場內關於班機延遲起飛的廣播、針對顧客的店內廣播等等。

新制多益
出題重點

常出的題目類型

- **What is the purpose of the announcement?**
  公告的目的為何？

- **What is the announcement mainly about?**
  公告主要與何事有關？

- **What will happen on/at（日期、時間等）?**
  在 XXX 的時候會發生何事？

- **What kind of event is taking place?**
  何種活動正在進行中？

- **What will the speaker most likely do next?**
  說話者接下來最有可能做什麼？

- **What does the speaker ask listeners to do?**
  說話者要求聽者做何事？

- **Where most likely is the announcement taking place?**
  公告最有可能在哪個地方進行？

- **What has caused a delay?**（內容為班機延遲起飛時）
  是什麼造成延遲？

- **What are listeners asked to do?**
  聽者被要求做何事？

- **What does the speaker encourage customers to do?**
  （店內廣播）
  說話者鼓勵消費者做何事？

 **talk（談話）**

內容與公告（announcement）或會議摘錄（excerpt from a meeting）相似的也不少，除此之外還會出與員工的談話、參觀美術館或工廠時的導覽、社內研修時的談話等等。

 **常出的題目類型**

● **What is the purpose of the talk?**

談話的目的為何？

● **Who most likely are the listeners?**

聽者最有可能是誰？

● **What will listeners do?**

聽者將要做何事？

● **Where is the talk most likely taking place?**

談話最有可能在哪個地方進行？

● **What are the listeners asked to do?**

聽者被要求做何事？

- **What will listeners receive later?**

  聽者接下來會收到什麼？

- **Who is the speaker?**

  說話者是誰？

- **What will be discussed after the talk?**

  話後將討論何事？

- **What has （公司名） recently introduces?**

  （○○公司）最近介紹了什麼？

 advertisement（廣告）

各式商品、服務的廣告，會出現各種行業的廣告，例如零售店、旅遊、不動產、銀行等等。內容與部分廣播（broadcast）中包含的廣告類似。

新制多益
出題重點

常出的題目類型

- **What is being advertised?**

  何物正在進行廣告？

- **Why should listeners visit a website?**

  為什麼聽者要去瀏覽網站？

● **Who is the intended audience for the advertisement?**

廣告的目標觀眾是誰？

● **What is the company offering this week?**

公司這週提供何物？

● **What is （公司名）known for?**

（○○公司）出名的地方是什麼？

TOEIC 聽力測驗

預想模擬試題

- 預想模擬試題的錄音在附屬音檔的Track 36 ~ 93。

- 請將書末的答案卡裁下，並使用答案卡作答。

- 解答及解析是從P176開始。

LISTENING TEST

This is the Listening part of the test, in which your comprehension of spoken English will be measured. The duration of the Listening test is about 45 minutes. Directions to each four parts of the Listening test will be provided. Be sure to mark your answers on the separate answer sheet. You must not write any answers in the test book.

PART 1

Directions: You will hear four comments about each picture in your test book. You must choose one comment that you feel best represents the picture for each question, and mark it on your answer sheet. Each comment will be said only once, and the comments are not shown in your test book.

Since comment (A), "They're having a meeting," best represents the picture, you should answer (A) by marking it on your answer sheet.

1.

2.

TURN TO THE NEXT PAGE

3.

4.

🎧 41-42

5.

6.

TURN TO THE NEXT PAGE ↘

PART 2

Directions: Here, a question or comment will be made and three replies will follow. These will be made only once and they will not be shown in your test book. After listening to the question or comment, on your answer sheet you must choose the best reply by marking (A), (B), or (C).

7. Mark your answer on your answer sheet.

8. Mark your answer on your answer sheet.

9. Mark your answer on your answer sheet.

10. Mark your answer on your answer sheet.

11. Mark your answer on your answer sheet.

12. Mark your answer on your answer sheet.

13. Mark your answer on your answer sheet.

14. Mark your answer on your answer sheet.

15. Mark your answer on your answer sheet.

16. Mark your answer on your answer sheet.

17. Mark your answer on your answer sheet.

18. Mark your answer on your answer sheet.

19. Mark your answer on your answer sheet.

20. Mark your answer on your answer sheet.

21. Mark your answer on your answer sheet.

22. Mark your answer on your answer sheet.

23. Mark your answer on your answer sheet.

24. Mark your answer on your answer sheet.

25. Mark your answer on your answer sheet.

26. Mark your answer on your answer sheet.

27. Mark your answer on your answer sheet.

28. Mark your answer on your answer sheet.

29. Mark your answer on your answer sheet.

30. Mark your answer on your answer sheet.

31. Mark your answer on your answer sheet.

TURN TO THE NEXT PAGE ↘

PART 1 照片描述

PART 2 應答問題

PART 3 簡短對話

PART 4 簡短獨白

TOEIC聽力測驗 預想模擬試題

PART 3

Directions: Here, conversations will take place between two or three people. Three questions will be shown regarding what was said in each conversation. You should choose what you feel is the correct response to each question by marking (A), (B), (C), or (D) on your answer sheet. Each part will be said only once, and will not be shown in your test book.

32. Who most likely is the woman?

(A) A hotel desk clerk
(B) A travel agent
(C) A gift shop manager
(D) An airline worker

33. What issue does the man mention?

(A) He has to collect his personal belongings.
(B) He needs to gain more customer points.
(C) He is in a hurry to reach a destination.
(D) He wants more information on a service.

34. What does the woman offer to send the man?

(A) An airport map
(B) An e-mail about a program
(C) A duty-free form
(D) An employee benefits package

35. What is the problem?

(A) Some staff require more training.
(B) Some tools are incorrect for a job.
(C) Some industrial equipment is broken.
(D) Some machines' delivery is overdue.

36. What is the man concerned about?

(A) A truck is too small to use.
(B) A task might be lengthy.
(C) A repair is only temporary.
(D) A utility company charges high rates.

37. What will the man probably do next?

(A) Borrow a company vehicle.
(B) Sign out of work for the day.
(C) Call two of his coworkers.
(D) Find a maintenance document.

38. What are the speakers mainly discussing?

(A) Going to Africa
(B) Creating designs
(C) Funding projects
(D) Putting on a talk

39. What does the woman mean when she says, "It's unclear whether we could put together any realistic plan for that"?

(A) A judgement is permanent.
(B) An organization lacks staff.
(C) A target is too unclear to reach.
(D) A proposal may be overly ambitious.

40. What will the man most likely do next?

(A) Serve the new menu.
(B) Gather some colleagues.
(C) Brainstorm with suppliers.
(D) Ask for public feedback.

TURN TO THE NEXT PAGE ↘

41. What is the purpose of the telephone call?

(A) To pay a bill
(B) To make a complaint
(C) To upgrade a service
(D) To set up an appointment

42. What does the woman ask the man for?

(A) A name
(B) An account code
(C) A telephone number
(D) A computer model

43. What benefit does the woman mention?

(A) A lower overall price
(B) A more secure ID
(C) A faster system
(D) An easier installation

....

44. Who most likely is the woman?

(A) A landscaper
(B) A property manager
(C) A housing investor
(D) A financial advisor

45. What does the woman say is required for a task?

(A) Interior building access
(B) A larger area
(C) Advanced skills
(D) A yearly audit

46. What does the woman suggest the man do?

(A) Become a regular client
(B) Oversee some complex work
(C) Confirm the quality of her staff
(D) Place an order before tomorrow

47. Why is the woman calling?

(A) To schedule a meeting.
(B) To talk about a manager.
(C) To ask about the progress of a project.
(D) To have her work reviewed by a committee.

48. What was the man preparing to do this afternoon?

(A) Spend time at a conference.
(B) Delete some outdated drafts.
(C) Update a computer program.
(D) Communicate with an executive.

49. What will the man do by 7 o' clock?

(A) Submit some of his work.
(B) Detail a financial proposal.
(C) Send a package to a coworker.
(D) E-mail some international vendors.

50. Where most likely does the woman work?

(A) At a public relations agency
(B) At a media firm
(C) At an event caterer
(D) At a department store

51. What did the woman do on Monday?

(A) Forwarded a list of services.
(B) Closed a deal with a food company.
(C) Transferred to another department.
(D) Attended a shareholder meeting.

52. What does the woman agree to do?

(A) Speak with her managers.
(B) Provide a sheet of questions.
(C) Clarify a shipment date.
(D) Meet a client in person.

TURN TO THE NEXT PAGE

53. What is the conversation mainly about?

(A) Reading literature
(B) Designing a paper
(C) Choosing electronics
(D) Getting repairs

54. Why is the man relieved?

(A) He can easily get a refund.
(B) He can avoid warranty fees.
(C) He is confident of the quality.
(D) He is paying a low price.

55. What does the woman ask the man to do?

(A) Select the best phone
(B) Choose a different brand
(C) Stay out of a closed aisle
(D) Follow her to another area

56. What is the conversation mainly about?

(A) Getting a delivery
(B) Buying cleaning items
(C) Choosing proper attire
(D) Finding a location

57. What is the man concerned about?

(A) Having a nice style
(B) Matching colors
(C) Saving money
(D) Getting a membership

58. What is implied will happen on May 4?

(A) An aisle will be renovated.
(B) A new store will open.
(C) A product line will arrive.
(D) A current sale will end.

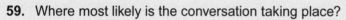

59. Where most likely is the conversation taking place?

(A) At an IT convention
(B) In a business office
(C) In a computer store
(D) At a systems seminar

60. What does Ralph suggest about the software?

(A) It appears to be complex.
(B) It lacks any online tutorial.
(C) It has to be installed soon.
(D) It has to use audio features.

61. What does the women say about monthly reporting?

(A) It uses up too many resources.
(B) It requires better software.
(C) Its operational speed has been affected.
(D) Its usual content has been taken offline.

TURN TO THE NEXT PAGE

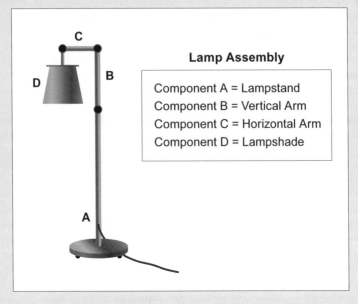

Lamp Assembly

Component A = Lampstand
Component B = Vertical Arm
Component C = Horizontal Arm
Component D = Lampshade

62. Where does the man most likely work?

(A) In sales
(B) In planning
(C) In customer service
(D) In accounting

63. Look at the graphic. What component is the woman missing?

(A) Component A
(B) Component B
(C) Component C
(D) Component D

64. When will the woman receive the component?

(A) In one day
(B) In three days
(C) In five days
(D) In seven days

65. Look at the graphic. What product is the woman disappointed about?

(A) Living room sets
(B) Dining room sets
(C) Bedroom furniture
(C) Kitchen cabinets

66. What does the man say is very difficult?

(A) Testing products
(B) Forming a team
(C) Making forecasts
(D) Hiring more staff

67. What is indicated about the Friday meeting?

(A) It will consider ways to manage costs.
(B) It will examine human resources operations.
(C) It will combine groups from several departments.
(D) It will include a quarterly review of performances.

TURN TO THE NEXT PAGE

Balano Foods

DISCOUNT COUPON

15% off

Yogurt (all brands)

Limit: 1 case

Expiration date: March 31

Usable in all states nationwide

68. Look at the graphic. Why is the coupon rejected?

(A) Because of the brands selected
(B) Because of the number of cases
(C) Because of the expiration date
(D) Because of state limits

69. What does the man say about the yogurt?

(A) He has considered it to be a favorite item.
(B) He has changed his mind about a restriction.
(C) He needs to confirm the new retail price.
(D) He wants to complain to store staff about it.

70. What most likely will the man do next?

(A) Choose a different food
(B) Get more dishware sets
(C) Go to a customer service area
(D) Buy a sheet of postage stamps

PART 4

Directions: Here, all spoken parts will be made by one speaker. You must answer three questions about what was said in each talk. You should choose what you feel is the correct response to each question by marking (A), (B), (C), or (D) on your answer sheet. Each part will be said only once, and will not be shown in your test book.

71. What is the radio broadcast about?

(A) A competition
(B) A job opening
(C) An education course
(D) A teaching policy

72. What restriction is mentioned in the radio broadcast?

(A) Work experience
(B) Age limits
(C) Assignment topics
(D) Investment rules

73. Why are listeners directed to a website?

(A) To buy gift certificates
(B) To view trophies
(C) To download stories
(D) To turn in projects

TURN TO THE NEXT PAGE ↘

74. Who most likely are the listeners?

(A) Company stock owners
(B) Financial regulators
(C) New employees
(D) Business reporters

75. According to the speaker, what has the company achieved this year?

(A) A rise in employee productivity
(B) Favorable coverage in the news
(C) Higher market share for the firm
(D) Record income for the business

76. Who will talk last?

(A) Nancy Fields
(B) Josh Gardner
(C) Mina Powers
(D) Gary Brooks

---

77. What is the news report mainly about?

(A) Local political elections
(B) Shopping mall construction
(C) A new facility that is opening
(D) A company marketing strategy

78. What is suggested about Plandar Technologies?

(A) It has applied for a number of new patents.
(B) It has encouraged the city to lower its taxes.
(C) It has numerous open career opportunities.
(D) It has a leading position in the IT industry.

79. According to the news report, what is a goal of Ms. Katz?

(A) Bringing additional firms to the area
(B) Adding more staff to the city government
(C) Recruiting more economists for planning
(D) Making a better effort to reach out to voters

🎧 87-88

PART 1 照片描述
PART 2 應答問題
PART 3 簡短對話
PART 4 簡短獨白
TOEIC聽力測驗 預想模擬試題

80. What is being advertised?

(A) A mortgage provider
(B) An accounting firm
(C) A real estate agency
(D) A debt collection business

81. According to the speaker, why would listeners choose this business?

(A) Its loans are large.
(B) Its service is fast.
(C) Its record is perfect.
(D) Its fees are reasonable.

82. What special offer is being made?

(A) Deposits are unnecessary.
(B) Packages arrive at no cost.
(C) Consultants work for free.
(D) Accounts are set up immediately.

....

83. What does the woman say has been taking place around the headquarters recently?

(A) The performance of renovation projects
(B) The expansion of some building areas
(C) The replacement of some old equipment
(D) The improvement of office supplies

84. What does the woman advise the listeners to do?

(A) Avoid some of the lower floors
(B) Bring in some items from home
(C) Meet later in the employee lounge
(D) Turn off the coffeemaker in the afternoon

85. What does the woman imply when she says, "This is something that we just have to get through"?

(A) A loss will be compensated for.
(B) A penalty will be endurable.
(C) A situation will be temporary.
(D) A business goal has to be reached.

TURN TO THE NEXT PAGE ↘

86. Why is the man calling?

(A) To respond to an earlier customer request

(B) To promote a special seasonal sale at the business

(C) To confirm the upcoming arrival date of a guest

(D) To outline the dates still open for reservations

87. Why would the listener have to pay an additional fee?

(A) To receive an accommodations change

(B) To have food and beverage room service

(C) To upgrade to faster wireless Internet service

(D) To have currency changed from dollars to pounds

88. What does the man offer to do?

(A) Replace a broken printer

(B) Wait for a customer e-mail

(C) Place a hold on a reservation

(D) Call back within the next two hours

....

89. What is the radio broadcast mainly about?

(A) The use of a zone for a project

(B) The sales of a recent movie release

(C) The operations budget of a firm

(D) The winners of a theater award

90. Who is Jessica Tan?

(A) An athletic star

(B) A police officer

(C) A security consultant

(D) An entertainer

91. What does the woman mean when she says, "Things here should be back to normal by Monday"?

(A) Mondays are usually routine.

(B) An event will be over.

(C) A service will be complete.

(D) The crowds will be satisfied.

92. What does the company want to focus on next year?

(A) Committing to finding new staff
(B) Developing new types of software
(C) Surveying shopping mall customers
(D) Entering potential new markets

93. What does the man imply when he says, "We want to establish whether this concept is truly realistic"?

(A) A proposal is unlikely to be accepted.
(B) Initial revenues are lower than expected.
(C) Research will verify the level of demand.
(D) Feedback from buyers has been limited.

94. What will all of the listeners receive in June?

(A) Lists of maintenance projects
(B) Information about client needs
(C) Results of ongoing repairs
(D) Ideas on future production plans

TURN TO THE NEXT PAGE ↘

RESTAURANTS WITH CATERING SERVICE	
Restaurant	Corporate Catering Discount
Paul's	10%
Everything Eats	12%
Wonder i-Chef	13%
Super Amaze	14%

95. What does the speaker remind the listeners about?

(A) Department reorganizations
(B) System errors
(C) Authorization levels
(D) Manager bonuses

96. Look at the graphic. What restaurant will the company choose?

(A) Paul's
(B) Everything Eats
(C) Wonder i-Chef
(D) Super Amaze

97. Why is the company looking forward to April 2?

(A) It will get exclusive product demands.
(B) It will have better website functionality.
(C) It will become more operationally efficient.
(D) It will improve the quality of its food.

🎧 93

PART 1 | 照片描述

PART 2 | 應答問題

PART 3 | 簡短對話

PART 4 | 簡短獨白

TOEIC聽力測驗 | 預想模擬試題

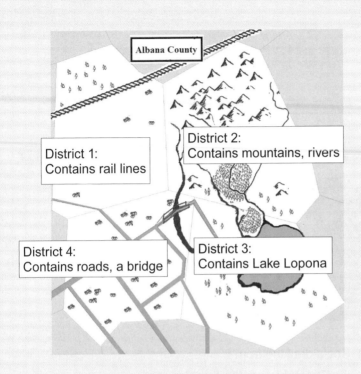

District 1:
Contains rail lines

District 2:
Contains mountains, rivers

District 4:
Contains roads, a bridge

District 3:
Contains Lake Lopona

Albana County

98. Where does the speaker work?

(A) At a government office
(B) At a property management business
(C) At an Internet retailer
(D) At an asset management firm

99. Look at the graphic. What district will be chosen?

(A) District 1
(B) District 2
(C) District 3
(D) District 4

100. What will the speaker do at the end of the meeting?

(A) Assign people to teams
(B) Take questions about plans
(C) Finalize a relocation schedule
(D) Contact the board of directors

預想模擬試題解答及解析

PART 1

1

> 只有1人登場
> →注意看動作！

(A) She's drinking from a cup.
(B) She's talking on the telephone.
(C) She's adjusting her chair.
(D) She's taking a book from a drawer.

(A) 她正用杯子喝東西。
(B) 她正在講電話。
(C) 她正在調整座椅。
(D) 她正從抽屜裡拿出一本書。

....

正確答案 (B)

照片中僅有1位女性，而描述該位女性動作的(B)即是正確答案。雖然「正在講電話」和「抽屜開著」等等都是Part 1中常出現的描述，但有drawer「抽屜」這個單字的(D)所使用的動詞與照片並不相符。

注釋

☐ adjust 調整　　　　　☐ drawer 抽屜

2 🎧 38

「人物」和「物品」兩方皆有登場→注意焦點放在「人」還是「物」。

(A) Some people are putting up signs near a door.
(B) Paintings have been hung in a large room.
(C) Furniture is being removed from a room.
(D) People are waiting to enter a building.

(A) 有些人正在門旁架立標誌。
(B) 畫作被掛在一個大房間裡。
(C) 傢俱正從一個房間裡搬離。
(D) 人們正等著進入一棟大樓。

正確答案　(B)

　　照片中印有「畫」和幾個「人」，題目的焦點可能放在畫上，也可能會放在人物身上。主詞為「人」且將焦點放在人物身上的句子是(A)和(D)，但這兩句與照片內容並不相符，而將焦點放在圖畫上的(B)則有正確描述照片。

注釋

☐ put up 架立　　☐ hang 掛、懸掛
☐ furniture 傢俱　☐ remove 搬離、去除

3

也可能會問僅有其中1人正在進行的動作！

(A) A woman is printing a document.
(B) Some people are facing each other.
(C) A man is operating a computer.
(D) Some books are stacked on the desk.

(A) 一名女子正在影印文件。
(B) 有些人面對彼此。
(C) 一名男子正在操作電腦。
(D) 有些書被疊放在桌上。

正確答案　(C)

雖然2個人都注視著電腦畫面，但並無描述2人共通點的句子，於是確認有沒有僅敘述其中1人動作的句子，便會發現只有男人正使用滑鼠操作電腦，因此(C)才是正確答案。

注釋

- □ document 文件
- □ operate 操作、運作
- □ face 面對、面向
- □ stack 疊放、堆疊

4 🎧 40

> 排成「一列」時句子中常會出現in a row！

(A) Some signs are being installed.

(B) Some cars are entering a repair shop.

(C) Some buildings are being painted.

(D) Some bicycles are parked in a row.

(A) 有些標示正在進行裝置。

(B) 有些車子正駛入一間維修店。

(C) 有些建築物正在進行油漆。

(D) 有些腳踏車被停成一排。

正確答案 (D)

照片中排放著腳踏車，正確描述出腳踏車的狀態及排列方式的 (D)便是正確答案。當腳踏車或汽車排成一列的時候，經常會使用in a row（排成一列）這種說法。

注釋

☐ install 安裝、裝設   ☐ repair shop 維修店
☐ park 停放（車）

5

「步道」叫做walkway。

🇨🇦 (A) A woman is standing on a balcony.

(B) Flowers and plants are aligned with a walkway.

(C) Bricks are piled next to a building.

(D) Wooden benches are being assembled.

(A) 一名女子站在陽台上。

(B) 花和植物對齊放在走道上。

(C) 磚塊被堆疊在建築物旁邊。

(D) 木板凳正被進行安裝。

正確答案 (B)

描述花朵與植物狀態的句子(B)有正確傳達出照片的內容。不只是花朵、植物，樹木、盆栽等的照片也經常被用來出題，walkway（步道、通道）這個單字也很常用到。

注釋

- balcony 陽台
- align 對齊
- brick 磚塊
- pile 堆放
- wooden 木製的
- assemble 組裝、聚集

6

人物相鄰的照片很常出！

 (A) Two women are seated beside each other.

(B) One of the women is opening her handbag.

(C) Some passengers are boarding a bus.

(D) One of the women is looking at her phone.

(A) 兩名女子坐在彼此旁邊。
(B) 其中一名女子正在打開她的手提包。
(C) 有一些旅客正在登上巴士。
(D) 其中一名女子正在看她的手機。

正確答案　(A)

正確答案 (A)

　　照片中2位女性相鄰而坐，所以正確答案是描述出這個情景的 (A)。相鄰而坐的照片經常用來出題，要描述「坐在一起」時常會使用sit beside each other、sit next to each other或sit side by side 這類說法。

注釋

□ seat 坐在～　　　□ beside 在～旁邊
□ passenger 乘客　　□ board 登上（車、船、飛機等）

PART 2

7　　　　　　　　　　　　　　　　　　　　

Do you know when the shipment will be sent?

(A) A large vessel.

(B) You'd better ask Adrien.

(C) Could you give me another choice?

你知道貨品什麼時候會出貨嗎？

(A) 一個大船。

(B) 你最好問亞德里安。

(C) 你可以給我另一個選擇嗎？

......

正確答案 (B)

　　這題是間接問句，必須聽到接在Do you know後面的when才行，然後回答(B)的話對話便能成立。近年針對以5W1H提問的題

目，像本題這樣不回答日期或地點，而是回答「你最好去問某某人」或是「這個現在不是我負責」的情形變得十分常見。

注釋

☐ shipment 貨品 ☐ vessel 船（艦）
☐ You'd(You had) better + 動詞原形　你最好～

8

A recent survey showed that staff would prefer a 4-day work week.

(A) It is closed on Sunday.
(B) Is the contract finished?
(C) I'd like to see the data.

近期的調查顯示，員工會偏好一個星期工作四天。
(A) 它星期日關門。
(B) 合約完成了嗎？
(C) 我想要看看數據。

....

正確答案　(C)

　　本題是以直述句回覆直述句的題目，需思考哪個回覆對母語者來說對話有自然展開。針對「近期的調查顯示，員工會偏好一個星期工作四天。」，回答(C)「想要看看數據」，便是相當自然的對話。由於這種題目變多了，所以題目和各個應答都得仔細聽才行。

☐ survey 調查　　☐ prefer 偏好　　☐ contract 合約

9

🇦🇺 You finished the presentation materials for tomorrow's meeting, didn't you?

🇬🇧 (A) I will call them later today.

(B) The schedule has not changed.

(C) No. I still have to make a few slides.

明天開會要用的簡報資料你做完了，對吧？

(A) 我今天晚點會打給他們。

(B) 時程表沒有更動。

(C) 還沒，還有幾張幻燈片得做。

....

正確答案　(C)

　　本題使用了「對吧？」這種向對方稍微尋求確認時使用的附加問句。針對「明天開會要用的簡報資料你做完了，對吧？」這個提問，回答(C)「還沒，還有幾張幻燈片得做」對話便會成立。

注釋

☐ material 資料　　☐ have to + 原形動詞　必須～

解答和解析

PART 1 照片描述

PART 2 應答問題

PART 3 簡短對話

PART 4 簡短獨白

TOEIC聽力測驗 預想模擬試題

10 47

 Why don't you go home and make a fresh start tomorrow?

(A) That sounds good. I'll do that.

(B) No, it hasn't arrived yet.

(C) It depends on the release date.

你何不先回家，明天再重新開始呢？

(A) 這聽起來不賴，就這麼辦。

(B) 不，它還沒到。

(C) 這取決於發表日。

....

正確答案 (A)

Why don't you ~?（你何不～？）是提議或邀請某事時經常使用的說法。針對「你何不先回家，明天再重新開始呢？」這個提議，回答(A)「這聽起來不賴，就這麼辦」對話便會成立。本題為用That's sounds good.（那聽起來不錯）或That is a good idea.（那是個好主意）來回覆提議的經典題目。

> **注釋**
> ☐ make a fresh start 重新開始
> ☐ depend on 取決於～　　☐ release date 發表日

11 48

Would you like to choose the restaurant for the banquet?

(A) The bank hours are 9 A.M. to 5 P.M.

(B) Sure. How about the new one on State Street?

(C) It was one of the finest presentations.

你想要選宴會的餐廳嗎？
(A) 銀行的營業時間是早上九點到傍晚五點。
(B) 當然，州街上新開的那間你覺得如何？
(C) 這是最好的簡報之一。

正確答案 **(B)**

Would you like to ~ ?的意思是「你想要～嗎？」，是比Do you want to ~?更為禮貌的說法。針對「你想選宴會的餐廳嗎？」這個提問，提議說「當然，州街上新開的那間你覺得如何？」的(B)是正確答案。像本題這樣以「提議」回覆提問的題目也常常會出。

注釋

□ banquet 宴會　　□ fine 良好的

12　　

How can we confirm the accuracy of the report?
(A) That's the legal team's responsibility.
(B) The reservation is for six people.
(C) We have decided to meet in person.

我們要如何確認報告的準確性？
(A) 那是法務團隊的工作。
(B) 預約人數是六個人。
(C) 我們決定親自見面。

正確答案 (A)

　　本題是詢問「方法」的How開頭疑問句，但不出示方法而是回答「那（不是我的工作而）是法務團隊的工作」的(A)才是正確答案。像本題這樣針對5W1H開頭的疑問句，回答「那是別人負責的事情」，也就是暗示「我不知道所以請去問負責的人」的題目也很常出。

注釋
□ confirm 確認
□ responsibility 責任
□ meet in person 親自見面
□ accuracy 準確性

13

🇨🇦 Would you mind meeting audience members after your presentation?

🇬🇧 (A) The auditorium has a new sound system.

　　(B) How many people are coming?

　　(C) The price of a membership will increase.

發表結束後，能請你和觀眾們見個面嗎？

(A) 禮堂有新的音響系統。

(B) 會來幾個人？

(C) 會員費用會增加。

正確答案 (B)

本題為Would you mind ~？（你介意～嗎？）開頭的請託句子。對於「發表結束後，能請你和觀眾們見個面嗎？」這個請託，雖然並未回答「好」或「不好」，但(B)「會來幾個人？」這樣的回答對母語者來說相當自然。

> **注釋**
>
> □ audience 觀眾　　　　□ auditorium 禮堂
> □ sound system 音響系統　□ membership 會員
> □ increase 增加

14

When is the company going to relocate its headquarters?

(A) Yes, she's been head of the firm since last quarter.
(B) It went very smoothly.
(C) It'll likely be sometime next year.

公司什麼時候要遷移總部？
(A) 是的，她從上一季開始就是公司的負責人。
(B) 事情非常順利。
(C) 很有可能是明年某個時候。

....

正確答案 (C)

針對When開頭的疑問句，回答sometime next year（明年某個時候）的(C)是正確答案。5W1H開頭的疑問句在近來的測驗中多半是採較有距離感的間接回應，不過本題卻是以往就有的形式，

是較為簡單的應答。(A)對於5W1H的疑問句,以Yes回答,所以是錯誤選項。

> **注釋**
>
> ☐ relocate 遷移　　☐ headquaters 總部
> ☐ head 負責人　　☐ quarter 季　　☐ smoothly 順利地
> ☐ likely 可能地　　☐ sometime 某個時候

15

🇨🇦 What was your major in university?

🇦🇺 (A) First in Pretoria, and then in Cape Town.
　　(B) No, it's not a major university.
　　(C) My focus was law.

你大學的主修是什麼?
(A) 先是普勒托利亞,接著是開普敦。
(B) 不,這不是一流的大學。
(C) 我專攻法律。

....

正確答案　(C)

　　本題的題目是在詢問大學時的「主修科目」,正確答案(C)之中使用和major不同的單字focus(專攻)來回覆。(B)使用了major企圖誤導考生,但內容卻未對應題目的提問,而且還用No來回答What開頭的疑問句,所以是錯誤選項。(A)則是被問到地點時的答覆,所以也是錯的。

注釋

☐ major 主修

16

🇺🇸 What catering service do you use for corporate events?

🇨🇦 (A) There'll be about 200 attendees.

(B) On October 18.

(C) We actually take care of those in-house.

在公司的活動中,你是叫哪裡的外燴?

(A) 大概會有 200 個參與人。

(B) 在 10 月 18 日。

(C) 事實上,我們是公司自己承辦的。

正確答案 (C)

　　針對「是叫哪裡的外燴?」這個問題,答案是(C)「事實上,我們是公司自己承辦的。」。像本題這樣,雖然沒有直接回應,但只要對話成立就是正確答案。(A)是用來回答How many開頭的問句,(B)則是用來回答When開頭的問句。

注釋

☐ catering service 外燴　　☐ corporate 企業的

☐ attendee 參與人　　☐ actually 事實上

☐ take care of 處理、照顧　　☐ in-house 內部的

17 🎧 54

We should take this car in for repairs.

(A) No, we don't need a pair.

(B) I know, it's not working well.

(C) That's an acceptable price.

我們應該要把這輛車帶去修理。

(A) 不，我們不需要一對。

(B) 我知道，它無法正常運作。

(C) 這是個可以接受的價格。

....

正確答案　(B)

　　本題是以直述句回答直述句，這類題目中「對話能自然開展的句子」就是答案。針對題目回答(B)，對話就會成立。(A)使用了和題目中的repairs（修理）發音相似的單字a pair（一對），企圖引誘考生選錯。(C)則是瞄準了只聽到題目中出現的repairs（修理）這個字的人，而「針對修理費用」回答，所以(C)和(A)一樣都是錯誤選項。

> **注釋**
>
> □ take~in 帶～去　　□ work 運作
> □ acceptable 可接受的

18 🎧 55

Who's going to decide on the supplier contract?

(A) You can contact me at my office.
(B) Our purchasing department.
(C) Yes, it's worth 200,000 euros.

誰將要在供應合約上做決策？
(A) 你可以在我的辦公室聯繫我。
(B) 我們的採購部門。
(C) 是的，它值 200,000 歐元。

正確答案　(B)

對於Who開頭的疑問句，經常會用部門來回答，算是比較簡單的題目。(A)用了和題目中的contract（合約）發音相似的單字contact（聯繫），企圖混淆視聽。(C)不但以Yes開頭，內容也和提問對不起來。

> **注釋**
>
> ☐ decide on 決定　　　☐ supplier 供應（商）
> ☐ purchasing department 採購部門　☐ worth 價值
> ☐ euro 歐元　　　　　☐ in-house 內部的

19

Where was the new photocopier installed?

(A) Because the old one kept breaking down.
(B) Yes, I'd like a copy of that photo.
(C) In the same spot as the old one.

新的影印機被安裝在哪裡？
(A) 因為舊的一直故障。

(B) 是的，我想要那張照片的影本。

(C) 和舊的同一個地方。

....

正確答案 (C)

　　對於Where開頭的問句，回答地點的(C)是正確答案。當題目用Where來問時，請記得只要選項裡有表示地點的前置詞in接上名詞的組合就是答案。由於Where不會用Because來回答，所以(A)是錯誤選項。(B)想要誤導考生，因此在句中使用了和題目中的photocopier（影印機）發音相似的photo（照片）。

注釋

☐ install 安裝　　☐ break down 故障　　☐ spot 地方

20

🇨🇦 Why are there so many tools spread out on the floor?

🇦🇺 (A) The delivery will be here soon.

(B) No, these stools aren't nailed to the floor.

(C) Sorry, I was just about to put them away.

為什麼地上灑落了這麼多工具？

(A) 配送很快就會到了。

(B) 不，這些凳子並沒有被釘在地上。

(C) 抱歉，我正要將它們歸位。

正確答案 (C)

　　本題是利用Why開頭的疑問句，來詢問工具散落一地的原因，(C)「抱歉，我正要把它們拿走」做為這個提問的回答，對話是成立的。就算不說出丟滿地的理由，回答「我馬上收拾」對母語者來說也是很自然的對話。

注釋

☐ tool 工具　　☐ spread out 散落　　☐ delivery 配送
☐ stool 凳子　　☐ nail 釘
☐ be about to + 原形動詞　正要～
☐ put away 歸位

21　　 58

Would you like me to bring you a menu?

(A) Yes, I'd appreciate that.
(B) It's been a fine meal, thank you.
(C) I meant to bring that to you.

你想要我拿菜單給你嗎？
(A) 是的，謝謝你。
(B) 這頓餐點很棒，謝謝你。
(C) 我有意把那個拿給你。

正確答案 (A)

　　Would you like me to ~?（你想要我～嗎？）這種題目也時常會出。當對方詢問意願時，可能會拜託對方，也可能會拒絕。在本題中，正確答案是回答「謝謝你」的(A)。錯誤選項(B)之中，為了誤導題目只聽到bring you a menu的人，而使用了可從menu（菜單）聯想到的meal（餐點）。

> **注釋**
>
> □ bring + 人 + 物　將物帶給人
> □ appreciate 感激；欣賞
> □ fine 良好的
> □ mean to + 原形動詞　有意要～

22　　

🇨🇦 What conference room should we use for the Friday meeting?

🇺🇸 (A) At 9:15 A.M. sharp.
　　(B) The one at the end of the hall.
　　(C) Yes, that's the right day.

我們星期五的會議要使用哪一間會議室？
(A) 早上九點十五分整。
(B) 走廊盡頭那一間。
(C) 是的，那是正確的日子。

- -

正確答案　(B)

　　正確答案是對於題目的「應該要用哪間會議室？」回答「走廊盡頭的那一間」的(B)。(B)中使用的代名詞one是指題目中提到的「會議室（conference room）」，像這樣在選項中用one來取代題目中使用的單字的情形十分常見。

23　

Where can I catch the shuttle bus to the airport?

(A) Right across the street.
(B) One comes about every 15 minutes.
(C) Yes, you can catch the ferry from that port.

我可以到哪裡搭接駁車去機場？
(A) 對街。
(B) 大約每隔十五分鐘就會有一班。
(C) 是的，你可以到那個港口搭渡輪。

正確答案　(A)

　　針對用詢問地點的疑問詞Where開頭的問句，出示地點的(A)就是正確答案。5W1H開頭的問句不能用Yes/No回答，所以(C)是錯誤選項，(B)則是因為對話接不上。

注釋

□ shuttle bus 接駁車　　□ every 每～
□ catch 搭乘

24

Do you normally take a subway line to your job?

(A) You can take it from this station.

(B) I'm an engineer.

(C) Yes, most of the time.

你通常都是搭地鐵線去上班的嗎？

(A) 你可以從這個站搭。

(B) 我是一名工程師。

(C) 是的，大多數時間都是。

....

正確答案 (C)

　　題目為一般問句，回覆可以用Yes/No也可以不用，所以無法當作提示，得仔細聽選項才行。對於「你通常都是搭地鐵去上班的嗎？」這個提問，選擇回答「大多數時間都是」的(C)就能讓對話成立。

> **注釋**
>
> □ normally 通常　　　　□ subway line 地下鐵線
>
> □ take 搭乘〜　　　　　□ engineer 工程師

25

 When will this sale end?

(A) Yes, almost everything in the store is 10 percent off.

(B) I sail whenever I get the chance.

(C) At the end of this week.

這場特賣什麼時候會結束？

(A) 是的，店裡幾乎所有商品都是九折。

(B) 我一有機會就會去航行。

(C) 這個週末。

....

正確答案　(C)

　　本題是用表示時間的疑問詞When開頭的問句，針對「這場特賣什麼時候結束？」這個提問，回答「這個週末」的(C)是正確答案。由於是直接回應，所以算是PART 2之中較容易答對的題目。5W1H起頭的疑問句不能用Yes/No回答，所以(A)是錯誤選項。(B)為了誤導考生，使用了和題目中用到的sale（特賣）發音相似的sail（航行）。

> **注釋**
>
> □ sale 特賣　　　　　　　　□ sail 航行
> □ whenever 每當～

26

🇨🇦 Aren't you with Coopers and Lin Assets?

🇦🇺 (A)　They've closed several big deals this year.

　　(B)　I am, in their human resources department.

　　(C)　Yes, we brought our tickets with us.

你不是在Coopers and Lin Assets上班嗎？

(A) 他們今年談成了幾筆大案子。

(B) 是的，我在他們的人資部門上班。

(C) 是的，我們有把票帶在身上。

正確答案 (B)

本題為Aren't開頭的否定問句，回答的方式和Are you開頭的問句相同。對於「你不是在Coopers and Lin Assets上班嗎？」，回答「是的，我在他們的人資部門上班」的(C)就是正確答案。(A)和(C)與話題內容對不上。

> **注釋**
>
> □ close a deal 完成交易、達成協議
> □ human resources department 人資部門

27

🇨🇦 These boots are a little tight on my feet.

🇺🇸 **(A) OK, I'll bring you a bigger size.**

(B) Yes, I agree they're a nice style.

(C) I'm glad that you like them.

這雙靴子穿在我的腳上有點緊。

(A) 好的，我會拿一雙大一點尺寸的給你。

(B) 是的，我同意他們的設計很不錯。

(C) 我很高興你喜歡它們。

正確答案 (A)

本題是用直述句回覆直述句的題目，在這類題目中「對母語者來說對話自然展開的選項」就是答案。對於題目的句子回覆(A)就能讓對話成立。(B)和(C)是為了誤導題目只有聽到其中一部分的人而設定的選項。

注釋

☐ tight 緊的　　　☐ agree 同意

28

🦘 Isn't Mr. Kim responsible for this project?

🇨🇦 **(A) Yes, as far as I know.**
　　(B) I'm all for it.
　　(C) Anytime he can.

是 Kim 先生負責這個企劃的，不是嗎？
(A) 對，就我知道的是這樣沒錯。
(B) 我非常贊同。
(C) 任何他可以的時間。

正確答案　(A)

　　這是用Isn't Mr. Kim開頭的否定問句，回答的方式和Is Mr. Kim 開頭的問句相同。對於題目的「是 Kim 先生負責這個企劃的，不是嗎？」，正確答案是回答「對，就我知道的是這樣沒錯」的 (A)。be responsible for ~（對～負責）和as far as I know（就我所知）都是PART 2中常用的講法。

注釋

☐ be all for 大力贊成
☐ anytime 任何時間

29

How can I best get in touch with you for any questions?

(A) **My mobile phone number is on my card.**
(B) I'd be happy to answer any that you might have.
(C) Thanks, but I don't have any questions at the moment.

有任何問題的話，我用哪種方式最能夠與你取得聯繫？
(A) 名片上有我的手機號碼。
(B) 我很樂意回答你可能會有的任何問題。
(C) 謝謝，但我目前沒有任何問題。

正確答案 (A)

這是個詢問有問題時要聯絡哪裡的問題，所以正確答案是回答「名片上有我的手機號碼」的(A)。為了誤導題目只聽到一部分的人，(B)的句子中使用了answer any。(C)則是想要引誘考生選錯，而使用了題目中出現過的單字questions。get in touch with ~（和~取得聯繫）這種說法在聽力部分的其他PART也時常使用。

注釋

□ mobile phone number 手機號碼　□ card 卡片；名片
□ I'd be happy to + 原形動詞　我很樂意~
□ at the moment 現在、當前

30

🇺🇸 Have Julia and Tom had a chance to review these spreadsheets?

🇨🇦 (A) I have, and they're accurate.

(B) Yes, but they're not finished.

(C) These sheets will look great on the bed.

統計表有機會讓Julia和Tom看過嗎？

(A) 我有看過了，它們是正確的。

(B) 有的，但是他們還沒看完。

(C) 這些床單在床上看起來會很漂亮。

正確答案 (B)

本題為一般問句，所以不管回應有沒有Yes/No都可以，請選出對母語者來說對話有自然展開的選項。對於「統計表有機會讓Julia和Tom看過嗎？」，選擇(B)「有的，但是他們還沒看完」就能讓對話成立。(A)的句子中用了題目出現過的單字have，而(C)則用了和spreadsheets發音相似的sheets（床單），企圖誘導考生。

> **注釋**
>
> ☐ review 審閱　　　　☐ spreadsheet 統計表
> ☐ accurate 準確的　　☐ look great on 在～上面很好看

31

 What kinds of music are you interested in?

(A) Yes, I'm very interested in music.

(B) Jazz, mostly, along with classical.

(C) Usually at concerts.

你對什麼類型的音樂有興趣？

(A) 是的，我對音樂非常有興趣。

(B) 主要是爵士樂，另外還有古典樂。

(C) 通常是在演唱會上。

正確答案 (B)

　　針對「你對什麼類型的音樂有興趣？」這個提問，(B)回答「主要是爵士樂，另外還有古典樂」。(A)的句子中原封不動地用了題目中出現過的片語interested in music，雖然偶爾也會有正確選項中使用和題目相同單字的情形，但幾乎不會整串片語直接使用，基本上會換句話說。(C)是為了誘導題目只聽到一部分的人而設的選項。

> **注釋**
>
> □ be interested in 對～有興趣
> □ mostly 大多是　　　　□ along with~ 附帶著～
> □ classical 古典的

PART 3

The next three questions, 32 to 34 relate to the following conversation.

W M

W: Thank you for staying with us, and I hope your time here was pleasant. But...uh... ① before you finish checking out, let me say that I noticed you're not a member of our loyalty program. If you join, you can collect points toward a free stay and other benefits. There's an application form right here.

M: Sounds interesting, but ② I've got to rush out to the airport, so I don't have time to fill that out.

W: That's OK. With your permission, ③ I could just send an e-mail with more information, and then you could decide for yourself whether or not you want to join. I'm sure that it'd be worthwhile for you.

對話內容中譯

32到34題題目與以下對話有關。

女：謝謝你住宿於此，希望你在這裡渡過的時光很愉快。但是……呃……①在你退房之前，讓我說明一下，我注意到你不是我們顧客忠誠計劃的會員。如果你加入的話，你可以集點擁有免費住宿和其他的福利。這裡就有一張申請表。

男：聽起來很有趣，②不過我要趕去機場了，所以我沒有時間填寫。

女：沒關係，一旦有你的許可，③我可以將更多資訊用電子郵件寄給你，那麼你便能自己決定是否要加入。我相信那對你來說會很值得。

32. Who most likely is the woman?

(A) **A hotel desk clerk**
(B) A travel agent
(C) A gift shop manager
(D) An airline worker

題目及選項中譯

32. 女子最有可能是誰？

(A) **一名旅館櫃檯人員**
(B) 一名旅遊業者
(C) 一名禮品店經理
(D) 一名航空作業員

正確答案　(A)

　　女性最初在底線①的部分提到「在你退房之前，讓我說明一下，我注意到你不是我們顧客忠誠計劃的會員」，所以可得知正確答案為 (A)。

33. What issue does the man mention?

(A) He has to collect his personal belongings.
(B) He needs to gain more customer points.
(C) **He is in a hurry to reach a destination.**
(D) He wants more information on a service.

題目及選項中譯

33. 男子提及到什麼問題？

(A) 他需要拿取他的私人物品
(B) 他需要得到更多消費點數
(C) **他正趕著要去目的地**
(D) 他想要一項服務更多的資訊

正確答案 **(C)**

在底線②的部分男性提到「不過我要趕去機場了,所以我沒有時間填寫」,所以正確答案為(C)。這題如果不知道題目中使用的 issue 有「問題」這個意思就可能無法答對。另外,(C)的句子裡將對話中使用到的 rush 替換成 be in a hurry。

....

34. What does the woman offer to send the man?
   (A) An airport map
   (B) An e-mail about a program
   (C) A duty-free form
   (D) An employee benefits package

題目及選項中譯

34. 女子提議要寄給男子什麼?
   (A) 一張機場地圖
   (B) 關於一個方案的電子郵件
   (C) 一張免稅表
   (D) 員工福利計畫

正確答案 **(B)**

底線③的部分女性提到「我可以將更多資訊用電子郵件寄給你」,由此可得知正確答案為(B)。只要有掌握從開頭開始整段對話的走向,就會知道選項中的 a program 是指最開始女性提到過的 a member of our loyalty program。

注釋

☐ pleasant 愉快的　　☐ loyalty program 顧客忠誠計劃
☐ benefit 福利　　　☐ application form 申請表

□ rush out to 趕去～
□ permission 允許、許可
□ personal belongings 私人物品
□ fill out 填寫
□ worthwhile 值得
□ destination 目的地

35-37

The next three questions, 35 to 37 relate to the following conversation.

W M

W: Ivan,① I need you to take these tools over to Building 21. Cassandra and Donald need them to repair one of the production machines there.

M: ② Sure, but that's pretty far away. It'll take me a while to walk there, drop these off, and then get back.

W: ③ Right, so I want you to take one of the company utility trucks. You can sign one of them out at the maintenance desk. Try to get back here within an hour, though. We're already getting... uh... quite busy with some production projects of our own.

M: It shouldn't be a problem. I'll be right back.

對話內容中譯

35到37題題目與以下對話有關。

女： 伊凡，①我需要你把這些工具拿到第二十一號大樓。卡珊卓和唐納德需要它們修裡那邊一個生產機器。

男： ②當然，但是那蠻遠的。我會需要花一點時間走到那裡、放下工具，然後再回來。

女： ③是的，所以我希望你用公司的公用車。你可以在維修櫃台那裡簽字領取。不過試著在一個小時內回來。我們已經開始……嗯……準備要開始為我們自己的生產計畫忙碌了。

男： 這應該不會是個問題。我會馬上回來。

35. What is the problem?

(A) Some staff require more training.

(B) Some tools are incorrect for a job.

(C) Some industrial equipment is broken.

(D) Some machines' delivery is overdue.

題目及選項中譯

35. 出現了什麼問題？

(A) 有些員工需要更多訓練

(B) 一個工作所使用的一些工具是不正確的

(C) 有些工業用設備故障了

(D) 有些機器延遲送達

正確答案　(C)

在開頭部分的底線①女性提到「需要你把這些工具拿到第二十一號大樓。卡珊卓和唐納德需要它們修裡那邊一個生產機器」，所以可得知將這個部分換句話說的(C)是正確答案。

....

36. What is the man concerned about?

(A) A truck is too small to use.

(B) A task might be lengthy.

(C) A repair is only temporary.

(D) A utility company charges high rates.

題目及選項中譯

36. 男子擔心的是什麼？

(A) 卡車太小無法使用

(B) 任務可能會很耗時

(C) 修理只是暫時的

(D) 水電公司的收費很高

正確答案 (B)

　　男性擔心的事情照理說會是男性本人提及，底線②的部分男性提到「當然，但是那蠻遠的。我會需要花一點時間走到那裡、放下工具，然後再回來。」由此可得知正確答案是(B)，不過如果不知道(B)裡面用到的lengthy（冗長的）這個單字，就選不出正確答案。

....

37. What will the man probably do next?

    (A) Borrow a company vehicle
    (B) Sign out of work for the day
    (C) Call two of his coworkers
    (D) Find a maintenance document

［題目及選項中譯］

37. 男子接下來有可能做什麼？

    (A) 借用一輛公用車
    (B) 當天暫停工作
    (C) 打電話給他的兩個同事
    (D) 找一個維修文件

正確答案 (A)

　　最後男性回說「這應該不會是個問題」，這必須去聽前面女性的發言，才有辦法理解是什麼事情沒問題。男性在底線②的部分擔心說「當然，但是那蠻遠的。我會需要花一點時間走到那裡、放下工具，然後再回來。」而女性在底線③的地方對此答說「是的，所以我希望你用公司的公用車。你可以在維修櫃台那裡簽字領取。」因此正確答案是(A)。題目用了probably，所以答案用推測的也沒關係。

38-40　🎧 72

The next three questions, 38 to 40 relate to the following conversation.

W　M

W: ① With our smaller budget, we might have to reduce the number of exhibitions that we hold next year... for example, the one we'd hoped to put on about West African masks.

M: There must be a way that we can avoid having to do that. ② Maybe we could fill that budget gap through fundraisers... uh... and other projects... uh... to raise donations.

W: ③ Ordinarily, I'd agree, but in order to meet our original exhibition plans, we'd have to raise 275,000 pounds before September 30. It's unclear whether we could put together any realistic plan for that.

M: I agree that'd be a real challenge... uh... but it's doable... and...

it's a service to the public. ④<u>Give me and my team a few days</u> <u>to brainstorm on this... uh... come up with a few ideas</u>.

對話內容中譯

38到40題題目與以下對話有關。

女：①<u>因為預算較少，我們可能需要減少明年舉辦的展覽數量</u>⋯⋯ 舉例來說，我們想要推出關於西非面具的那個展覽。

男：一定有一個方式能讓我們避免這麼做。②<u>或許我們可以透過募資</u> <u>來補足預算缺口</u>⋯⋯嗯⋯⋯<u>或是其他企畫</u>⋯⋯嗯⋯⋯<u>來募款</u>。

女：③<u>通常來說，我會同意，但是為了符合我們原初的展覽計畫，</u> <u>我們需要在九月三十日前募到 275,000 磅。</u>我們能否為了達 標而擬定任何實際方案仍不清楚。

男：我同意這會是的真正的挑戰⋯⋯嗯⋯⋯但是這是可行的⋯⋯而 且⋯⋯這是為大眾服務。④<u>給我和我的團隊幾天來針對這件事</u> <u>進行腦力激盪</u>⋯⋯想出幾個點子。

---

38. What are the speakers mainly discussing?
(A) Going to Africa
(B) Creating designs
(C) Funding projects
(D) Putting on a talk

題目及選項中譯

38. 說話者主要是在討論什麼？
(A) 去非洲
(B) 進行設計
(C) 募資計畫
(D) 舉行一場演講

正確答案 (C)

　　本題是提示會出現好幾次的類型。底線①提到「因為擁有較少的預算，我們可能需要減少明年舉辦的展覽數量」，接下來的發言則對此提議「一定有一個方式能讓我們避免這麼做。或許我們可以透過募資來補足預算缺口」，後面的對話又再進一步闡述意見。因此，正確答案為(C)。

....

39. What does the woman mean when she says, "It's unclear whether we could put together any realistic plan for that"?

(A) A judgment is permanent.
(B) An organization lacks staff.
(C) A target is too unclear to reach.
(D) A proposal may be overly ambitious.

39. 當女子說「我們能否為了達標而擬定任何實際方案仍不清楚。」時，是什麼意思？

(A) 一項判決是具永久性的
(B) 一間機構缺少員工
(C) 一個目標過於不明確以至於難以達到
(D) 一項提案可能過於有野心

正確答案 (D)

　　本題為詢問意圖題。這種類型的題目連「」前面的對話也得仔細聽，必須了解話題的走向才有辦法作答。底線②的地方男性提起要不要募款，接著在底線③的地方女性對此表示「通常來説，我會同意，但是為了符合我們原初的展覽計畫，我們需要在九月三十日

前募到 275,000 磅」，由於是順著這個接續下去的對話，所以考量話題的走向便可得知正確答案為(D)。

---

40. **What will the man most likely do next?**

    (A) Serve the new menu.
    (B) Gather some colleagues.
    (C) Brainstorm with suppliers.
    (D) Ask for public feedback.

> **題目及選項中譯**

40. 男子接下來最有可能做什麼？

    (A) 提供新菜單
    (B) 召集一些同事
    (C) 與供應商腦力激盪
    (D) 要求大眾回饋

正確答案　(B)

    What will the man / the woman do next?是第3小題常出的題目，而且因為題目中有表示未來的will，所以可得知答案會出現在對話的後半。對話最後的底線④提到「給我和我的團隊幾天來針對這件事進行腦力激盪」，所以將這個部分換句話説的(B)即是正確答案。

注釋

- [ ] budget 預算
- [ ] put on 舉辦
- [ ] gap 缺口、裂縫
- [ ] raise donations 募款
- [ ] pound 磅（英國貨幣單位）
- [ ] unclear 不清楚的、不明確的
- [ ] put together 組合、組織在一起
- [ ] doable 可行的
- [ ] brainstorm 腦力激盪
- [ ] come up with 想出、思考出
- [ ] funding 資金
- [ ] lack 缺少
- [ ] overly 過度地
- [ ] serve 提供、服務
- [ ] colleague 同事

- [ ] exhibition 展覽   [ ] hold 舉辦
- [ ] fill 填補、填入
- [ ] fundraiser 募資
- [ ] ordinarily 通常

- [ ] permanent 長期的、永久的
- [ ] proposal 提案
- [ ] ambitious 具有野心的
- [ ] gather 聚集、集合
- [ ] supplier 供應商

41-13

 73

The next three questions, 41 to 43 relate to the following conversation.

🇨🇦 M   🇦🇺 W

M: Hello, I'm calling about my telecom service. ① I'm only buying Internet service from your company now, but I'd like to add mobile phone and cable TV to that.

W: I'd be happy to arrange that for you. ② Can I have your account ID please?

M: I don't have that right in front of me, but my name is Mark Lee and my phone number is 303-555-9472.

214

W: Okay, I see your name in our computer system. I can easily make the change for you right away. ③ <u>The added fee for this service would be an additional 45 dollars per month—still 20 percent off what it would cost if purchased separately.</u>

對話內容中譯

41到43題題目與以下對話有關。

男：嗨，我來電是想詢問我的電信服務。①<u>我現在只有購買貴公司的網路服務，但是我想要增加手機和有線電視服務。</u>

女：我很樂意為您安排。②<u>請給我您的帳戶名稱好嗎？</u>

男：我現在沒有，但是我的名字是李馬克，我的電話號碼是 303-555-9472。

女：好的，我有在我們的電腦系統裡看見你的名字了。我現在可以立刻幫您更改。③<u>此服務的新增費用會是每個月多收 45 元——但仍然比分開購買還要便宜 20 ％。</u>

41. **What is the purpose of the telephone call?**
   (A) To pay a bill
   (B) To make a complaint
   (C) To upgrade a service
   (D) To set up an appointment

題目及選項中譯

41. 此通來電的目的為何？
   (A) 付帳單
   (B) 提出申訴
   (C) 升級服務
   (D) 安排會面

正確答案　(C)

　　詢問打電話目的的題目很常會出，打電話的目的多半會在開頭

部分陳述，所以開頭的地方要特別注意。底線①男性提到「我現在只有購買貴公司的網路服務，但是我想要增加手機和有線電視服務」，所以正確答案為(C)。

....

42. What does the woman ask the man for?

    (A) A name

    (B) An account code

    (C) A telephone number

    (D) A computer model

題目及選項中譯

42. 女子要求男子提供什麼？

    (A) 姓名

    (B) 帳戶名稱

    (C) 電話號碼

    (D) 電腦模型

正確答案　(B)

女性詢問的內容理論上會在女性自己的發言之中，底線②的地方提到「請給我您的帳戶名稱好嗎？」所以可得知正確答案是(B)。

....

43. What benefit does the woman mention?

    (A) A lower overall price

    (B) A more secure ID

    (C) A faster system

    (D) An easier installation

題目及選項中譯

43. 女子提及了什麼福利？

(A) 較低的總價

(B) 更有保障的帳戶名稱

(C) 更快的系統

(D) 更簡單的安裝

正確答案　(A)

　　底線③的地方女性提到「此服務的新增費用會是每個月多收 45 元──但仍然比分開購買還要便宜 20 %。」所以將這部分換句話說的(A)就是正確答案。

注釋

☐ telecom service 電信服務
☐ account 帳戶
☐ fee 費用
☐ per month 每一個月
☐ separately 分開地
☐ complaint 抱怨
☐ upgrade 升級
☐ appointment 會面、見面
☐ overall 整體的
☐ additional 額外的
☐ benefit 福利
☐ installation 安裝

The next three questions, 44 to 46 relate to the following conversation.

W M

W: Mr. Kim, here's the estimate for taking care of the entire grounds of the building: 700 euros. ① That includes trimming the bushes, laying down new seed and fertilizer, and grass cutting.

M: I was hoping to get this done for less than 500 euros. I don't think the area around this office building is really that large.

W: ② It's not just the size of the area... uh... it's complex to properly trim the type of tall bushes you have. To be frank, ③ I'd recommend a yearly service agreement... that way we could make sure your grounds are always perfect.

M: I'll check the quality of the work that you do this time. If it's good, we may order it again.

對話內容中譯

44到46題題目與以下對話有關。

女： 金先生，這裡是照料整個大樓地面的估價：700歐元。①這包含修剪草叢、種新的種子和施肥，以及剪草。

男： 我是希望可以用低於 500 歐元的價錢把這件事做好。我不覺得這棟辦公大樓附近的區域真的有那麼大。

女： ②這不單單只是地區大小的問題……嗯……要恰當地修剪你種的高灌木叢是很複雜的。老實說，③我想要推薦你一個年度服務合約……那樣一來，我們就可以確保你的土地看起來總是完美無瑕。

男： 我會先確認你這次施工的品質。如果很好的話，我們會再訂購服務。

44. Who most likely is the woman?

(A) A landscaper
(B) A property manager
(C) A housing investor
(D) A financial advisor

題目及選項中譯

44. 女子的身分最有可能為何？

(A) 園藝業者
(B) 房地產經理人
(C) 不動產投資者
(D) 財經顧問

正確答案　(A)

　　本題是會有好幾次提示的類型，光是在女性最初的發言底線①的部分，提示就出現了好幾次。由於提到「包含修剪草叢、種新的種子和施肥，以及剪草」，所以由此可知從事這些工作的是(A)「園藝業者」。

45. What does the woman say is required for a task?

(A) Interior building access
(B) A larger area
(C) Advanced skills
(D) A yearly audit

題目及選項中譯

45. 女子說明此份工作需要什麼？

(A) 進入到建築物內部
(B) 一塊大的區域
(C) 高超的技巧
(D) 年度審查

正確答案 (C)

　　最開始女性出示估價金額，對此男性表示「希望能降到500歐元以下」。對於認為金額過高的男性，女性在底線②的地方回答「這不單單只是地區大小的問題……嗯……要恰當地修剪你種的高灌木叢是很複雜的。」，所以可得知正確答案為(C)。

··

46.　**What does the woman suggest the man do?**

　　(A) Become a regular client
　　(B) Oversee some complex work
　　(C) Confirm the quality of her staff
　　(D) Place an order before tomorrow

題目及選項中譯

46. 女子建議男子做什麼？

　　(A) 成為固定的客戶
　　(B) 監督一些複雜的工作
　　(C) 確認她的員工的品質
　　(D) 明天前下單

正確答案 (A)

　　女性在底線③的地方說「我想要推薦你一個年度服務合約……那樣一來，我們就可以確保你的土地看起來總是完美無瑕。」，所以正確答案是(A)。題目中用到了suggest，不過在對話中用的卻是recommend，要小心這種代換說法的地方。

注釋

□ estimate 預估　　□ include 包含
□ lay down 放置　　□ fertilizer 肥料

- ☐ properly 合適地、適切地
- ☐ recommend 推薦
- ☐ agreement 合約、契約、協定
- ☐ interior 內部的
- ☐ advanced 高超（階）的、進階的
- ☐ audit 審查
- ☐ oversee 監督
- ☐ place an oder 下單
- ☐ to be frank 老實說
- ☐ yearly 每年地
- ☐ destination 目的地
- ☐ regular 固定的、定期的
- ☐ confirm 確認

47-49

 75

The next three questions, 47 to 49 relate to the following conversation.

W M

W: John, this is Valeria Sanchez, the new editor over at Fast Data Magazine. I'm wondering if you have a moment to chat about your work.

M: ② I was just getting ready to conduct an e-mail interview with a CIO this afternoon... uh... for one of your articles. But I've got a few minutes.

W: Good. ① I've seen some of your work updates, but I'm wondering if I could see full drafts of what you're working on... eh... just to make sure they're going in the right direction.

M: I'd want to make a few changes... that is... uh... add a few more details, cut some parts, and so on... but ③ I can have those over to you by around 7 o'clock this evening. All I need is the e-mail address that I should send them to.

47到49題題目與以下對話有關。

女：約翰，我是瓦萊里婭‧桑切斯，《快數據雜誌》的新編輯。我在想你是否有時間聊聊你的工作。

男：②我正準備要和 CIO 在下午進行電子郵件面試⋯⋯嗯⋯⋯為了你的一篇文章。但我有幾分鐘的時間。

女：很好。①我已經有看了幾篇你的工作更新，但是我在想我能不能看看你現正著手的完整草稿⋯⋯呃⋯⋯就是確認一下文章的方向是對的。

男：我想要做幾個修改⋯⋯就是⋯⋯呃⋯⋯加一些細節，刪減掉一些地方，等等⋯⋯但是③我可以在晚上七點左右把那些文章傳給你。我需要一個可以把文章寄過去的電子郵件。

---

47. **Why is the woman calling?**
   (A) To schedule a meeting
   (B) To talk about a manager
   (C) To ask about the progress of a project
   (D) To have her work reviewed by a committee

題目及選項中譯

47. 為什麼女子要來電？
   (A) 替會議安排時間
   (B) 談論關於一名經理
   (C) 詢問專案的進度
   (D) 將她的作品給一名委員審理

正確答案 (C)

　　雖然打電話的目的大多會在開頭部分提及，但要答出本題卻需要多聽一點並掌握到對話的走向。最初身為編輯的女性問說「我在想你是否有時間聊聊你的工作」，然後男性回答「我有幾分鐘的時

間」，之後的對話女性在底線①提到「我已經有看了幾篇你的工作更新，但是我在想我能不能看看你現正著手的完整草稿……呃……就是確認一下文章的方向是對的。」，所以將這部分統整起來的(C)就是正確答案。

48.　What was the man preparing to do this afternoon?
(A)　Spend time at a conference
(B)　Delete some outdated drafts
(C)　Update a computer program
(D)　Communicate with an executive

> 題目及選項中譯

48. 男子準備要在這個下午做什麼？
(A) 參加會議
(B) 刪除舊的檔案
(C) 更新電腦系統
(D) 與一名高階主管談話

正確答案　(D)

　　題目中的this afternoon是關鍵字，因為題目的主詞是the man，所以要注意聽男性的發言，底線②的地方就出現了這個this afternoon。題目是詢問男性在準備什麼，所以要注意聽那個部分，由於他提到「我正準備要和 CIO 在下午進行電子郵件面試」，因此將這個部分換句話說的(D)就是正確答案。

49. What will the man do by 7 o' clock?

(A) Submit some of his work.
(B) Detail a financial proposal.
(C) Send a package to a coworker.
(D) E-mail some international vendors.

49. 七點的時候男子會做什麼？

(A) 提交他的一些作品
(B) 將一份金融提案加入細節
(C) 將一份包裹寄給同事
(D) 寄信給國際賣方

正確答案 (A)

　　題目中的7 o'clock是關鍵字，由於題目的主詞是the man，所以可推測出可能是男性會回答，最後男性的發言中就有出現7 o'clock。底線③的地方提到「我可以在晚上七點左右把那些文章傳給你。我需要一個可以把文章寄過去的電子郵件。」，所以(A)就是正確答案。

注釋

- □ editor 編輯
- □ get ready to do 準備好做～
- □ CIO(Chief Information Officer) 資訊總監
- □ fundraiser 募資
- □ update 更新
- □ make sure (that) 確認
- □ schedule 將……排入時程
- □ review 複審、評論
- □ outdated 過時的；舊式的
- □ detail 細節
- □ chat 聊天；談話
- □ conduct 執行、實施
- □ article 文章
- □ draft 草稿
- □ direction 方向
- □ progress 進展
- □ vendor 賣主

50-52 76

The next three questions, 50 to 52 relate to the following conversation with three speakers.

W M-1 M-2

W: Hello, I'm Katherine Heinz from Lucko-Gordon Partners. I'm calling for Mr. Dunne in Operations.

M-1: Can I ask what it's about?

W: ① It's about your company's upcoming shareholder meeting. We'll be providing food and beverages for it.

M-1: Oh, yes, he's expecting your call on that. Please hold for a moment, while I check to see if he's in. If he is, I'll transfer you.

M-2: Katherine? ② You called at the perfect time. I was just going over the price and service sheet that you e-mailed me on Monday.

W: I hope it's satisfactory.

M-2: For the most part, it is. I do have a few questions about some of the items. ③ I'd like you to clarify them, but here in our offices.

W: ④ That'd be no problem. Just tell me a date and time when you're available to meet.

對話內容中譯

50到52題目與以下三人之間的對話有關。

女：你好，我是鹿口－高登合夥公司的凱薩琳‧海恩茲。我打來是要找營運部門的鄧恩先生。

男一：可以詢問是什麼事宜嗎？

女：①是關於貴公司接下來的股東會議。我們將會準備食物和飲品。

男一：噢，對，他正在等你打電話來。請稍等一下，我去看看他在不在。如果他在的話，我再幫您轉接。

225

男二：凱薩琳？②你打來的正是時候。我正在審閱你星期一寄給我的價格和服務表。

女：我希望你很滿意。

男二：大部分是很滿意的。不過我對一些物件有幾個問題。③我希望你能闡述一下，但是是在我們辦公室。

女：④那沒有問題。只要你告訴我一個你有空會面的日期和時間。

....

50. **Where most likely does the woman work?**
    (A) At a public relations agency
    (B) At a media firm
    (C) At an event caterer
    (D) At a department store

題目及選項中譯

50. 女子最有可能在哪裡工作？
    (A) 公關公司
    (B) 媒體公司
    (C) 活動外燴
    (D) 百貨公司

正確答案 (C)

　　女性在底線①的地方提到「是關於貴公司接下來的股東會議。我們將會準備食物和飲品」，所以可得知正確答案為(C)。本題為3人對話題，有2位男性登場。打電話來的女性是外燴公司的人，而2位男性中的其中1人是接起自女性的電話的人，另1位則是電話轉接後接電話的人。

51. What did the woman do on Monday?

(A) Forwarded a list of services
(B) Closed a deal with a food company
(C) Transferred to another department
(D) Attended a shareholder meeting

題目及選項中譯

51. 女子在星期一做了什麼？

(A) 轉寄了一份服務清單
(B) 與一間食品公司簽約
(C) 轉調去其他部門
(D) 參加股東會議

正確答案 (A)

題目的Monday是關鍵字。女性打電話來確認即將舉辦的股東會要用的外燴服務，對此男性負責人在底線②部分表示「你打來的正是時候。我正在審閱你星期一寄給我的價格和服務表」，由此可得知女性是在星期一寄的電子郵件，所以正確答案為(A)。

52. What does the woman agree to do?

(A) Speak with her managers
(B) Provide a sheet of questions
(C) Clarify a shipment date
(D) Meet a client in person

52. 女子同意做什麼？

　　(A) 與她的主管談話

　　(B) 提供問題表

　　(C) 說明運送日期

　　(D) 與客戶見面

正確答案　(D)

　　女性同意的內容照理說會出現在女性本人的發言之中。男性在底線③的地方提到「我希望你能闡述一下，但是是在我們辦公室」，接著女性在底線④的部分表示「那沒有問題。只要你告訴我一個你有空會面的日期和時間」，因此正確答案為(D)。in person 的意思是「親自」，在TOEIC聽力部分經常會出現。

注釋

- [ ] upcoming 即將到來的
- [ ] shareholder meeting 股東會議
- [ ] provide 提供
- [ ] beverage 飲料、飲品
- [ ] expect 期待
- [ ] transfer 轉調
- [ ] go over 查看
- [ ] satisfactory 令人滿意的
- [ ] close a deal 簽約
- [ ] clarify 澄清、闡述
- [ ] available 有空的
- [ ] forward 轉寄
- [ ] transfer to 轉調至～
- [ ] shipment date 運輸日
- [ ] in person 親自

53-55

 77

The next three questions, 53 to 55 relate to the following conversation.

🇬🇧 M 🇦🇺 W

M: Hello, ① I'm looking for an electronic reader. I'd be willing to pay a little more for something good... er... thin, light, and with long battery life, too.

W: We have a number of items like that. Did you have a particular brand in mind?

M: ② I'd like to have a look at some of your best ones. That is... I... uh... really want something that's going to last for quite a while.

W: I'm sure that I can find you something like that. ③ Nearly all of the best units have 9-month warranties, too, so you'll be assured you have something that's worth the price.

M: ④ I'm relieved to hear that. That way I'll know that... uh... it won't fall apart on me early on. And even if it did, I could get it fixed for free.

W: Absolutely. ⑤ Please come with me over to Aisle 19. You can look over what we have there... and see which one you like best.

對話內容中譯

53到55題題目與以下對話有關。

男：哈囉，①我想要找一個電子閱讀器。我願意多花一點錢買好一點的東西⋯⋯呃⋯⋯薄、輕，以及電池續航力久。

女：我們有很多類似的產品。你有特別想要哪一個品牌嗎？

男：②我想要看看你們最好的幾個產品。就是⋯⋯我⋯⋯呃⋯⋯真的想要可以用比較久的產品。

女：我很確定我可以幫你找到你要的產品。③幾乎所有最好的產品也都有九個月的保固，所以你可以放心你買到值得這個價格的產品。

男：④<u>聽到這個我很欣慰。那樣的話我就知道⋯⋯呃⋯⋯它不會剛</u>開始用就壞掉。而且就算真的壞了，我也可以拿去免費維修。

女：當然。⑤<u>請跟我到第十九道。你可以看看我們那裡的產品⋯⋯</u><u>然後看看你最喜歡哪個。</u>

···

53. What is the conversation mainly about?

(A) Reading literature
(B) Designing a paper
(C) Choosing electronics
(D) Getting repairs

題目及選項中譯

53. 對話主要是關於什麼？

(A) 閱讀文學
(B) 設計紙張
(C) 選擇電器產品
(D) 進行修繕

正確答案　(C)

　　這是第1小題常出的題型，可能會像這題一樣問說What is the conversation mainly about?（對話主要是關於什麼？），也可能會問What are the speakers discussing?（說話者在討論什麼？），且提示會出現數次。在男性最初的發言（底線①）中提到「我想要找一個電子閱讀器。我願意多花一點錢好一點的東西⋯⋯呃⋯⋯薄、輕，以及電池續航力久」，由此可知正確答案為(C)。

···

54. Why is the man relieved?

(A) He can easily get a refund.
(B) He can avoid warranty fees.

(C) He is confident of the quality.

(D) He is paying a low price.

題目及選項中譯

54. 男子為什麼感到欣慰？

(A) 他可以輕易拿到退款

(B) 它可以避免保固費用

(C) 他對品質很有信心

(D) 他付了低價

正確答案 (C)

　　男性在底線④的地方提到I'm relieved to hear that.（聽到這個我很欣慰），而這個that指的就是這之前女性的發言內容。在更前面的男性發言之中也有提示。男性在底線②的地方説「我想要看看你們最好的幾個產品。就是……我……呃……真的想要可以用比較久的產品」，接著女性在底線③的地方表示「幾乎所有最好的產品也都有九個月的保固，所以你可以放心你買到值得這個價格的產品」，因此正確答案為(C)。

....

55. What does the woman ask the man to do?

(A) Select the best phone

(B) Choose a different brand

(C) Stay out of a closed aisle

(D) Follow her to another area

題目及選項中譯

55. 女子要求男子做什麼？

(A) 選擇最好的手機

(B) 選擇不同的品牌

(C) 遠離已關閉的走道

(D) 跟著她到另一個區域

正確答案 (D)

請託的內容應該會出現在題目主詞的女性的發言之中。最後女性提到「跟我到第十九道。你可以看看我們那裡的產品……然後看看你最喜歡哪個。」（底線⑤），所以可得知正確答案為(D)。

注釋

- [ ] electronic reader 電子閱讀器
- [ ] be willing to do 願意去做～
- [ ] a number of 若干
- [ ] particular 特定的
- [ ] have~in mind 有～想法
- [ ] have a look at 看一看、審視
- [ ] for quite a while 一段時間
- [ ] warranty 保固
- [ ] be assured that 可以被保證～
- [ ] be relieved to do 鬆了一口氣，可以去～
- [ ] fall apart 壞掉、故障
- [ ] early on 早期
- [ ] get~fixed 將～拿去修
- [ ] aisle 走道
- [ ] look over 檢查
- [ ] literature 文學
- [ ] electronics 電器產品
- [ ] get a refund 得到退款
- [ ] warranty fee 保固費
- [ ] be confident of 對～有信心
- [ ] stay out of 遠離

56-58

 78

The next three questions, 56 to 58 relate to the following conversation.

🇨🇦 M 🇺🇸 W

M: Excuse me, ① I'm looking for a suit jacket. It has to be formal, for my work.

W: I see. Have you considered buying a pair of pants to go with it? If you buy it separately later on, the color or style might not match the jacket.

M: Hmm... you could be right. ② I'll consider buying a complete suit, as long as I can get something that's on sale.

W: Well, ③ we have quite a few pieces that are, at least until May 4. Also, you don't need a store membership.

M: In that case, I'm certainly interested.

W: I'm happy to hear that. Please follow me over to Aisle 10, and I'll show you what we have.

對話內容中譯

56 到 58 題題目與以下對話有關。

男：不好意思，①我正在找一件西裝外套。它必須要是正式的，工作用的。

女：我明白。你有考慮過買一套褲子來搭配它嗎？如果你之後才單獨買，它的顏色或風格可能不會和外套相搭。

男：嗯……也許你是對的。②我會考慮買一整套西裝，只要能買到特價的。

女：這樣啊，③我們有不少套是特價的，特價到五月四號。除此之外，你不需要有店家會員。

男：這樣的話，那我當然有興趣。

女：我很高興聽到你這麼說。請跟我到走道十，我會向你展示我們的商品。

56. What is the conversation mainly about?

(A) Getting a delivery
(B) Buying cleaning items
(C) Choosing proper attire
(D) Finding a location

題目及選項中譯

56. 對話是關於什麼？

(A) 提供交付
(B) 買清潔產品
(C) 選擇合適的服裝
(D) 尋找地點

正確答案 (C)

　　這種類型的題目，答案經常出現在開頭部分。就算錯過了開頭部分，多數情況下，提示多半會出現好幾次。男性在最初的發言（底線①）提到「正在找一件西裝外套。它必須要是正式的，工作用的」，所以正確答案為(C)。

57. What is the man concerned about?

(A) Having a nice style
(B) Matching colors
(C) Saving money
(D) Getting a membership

題目及選項中譯

57. 男子擔心的是什麼？

(A) 擁有好的風格

(B) 顏色搭配

(C) 省錢

(D) 取得會員資格

正確答案 **(C)**

主詞是the man，所以應該會是男性回答。底線②的地方男性說到「我會考慮買一整套西裝，只要能買到特價的」，所以正確答案為(C)。

....

58. What is implied will happen on May 4?

    (A) An aisle will be renovated.

    (B) A new store will open.

    (C) A product line will arrive.

    (D) A current sale will end.

題目及選項中譯

58. 什麼事情被暗示會發生在五月四日？

    (A) 一個走道將進行翻修

    (B) 一間新店將開幕

    (C) 一個產品線將抵達

    (D) 一個近期的特賣將結束

正確答案 **(D)**

May 4是關鍵字，得注意聽May 4。男性在底線②的地方提到「會考慮買一整套西裝，只要能買到特價的」，對此女性在底線③的地方回答「我們有許多套是特價的，特價到五月四號」，由此可知正確答案為(D)。題目裡用了imply（暗示）這個字，所以只要是可由對話推測出來的都可以作為答案。

59-61

The next three questions, 59 to 61 relate to the following conversation with three speakers.

🇬🇧 W 🇦🇺 W-1 🇺🇸 W-2

M: Ellen, I'm struggling a little bit trying to understand this new accounting software that was installed yesterday. How about you?

W-1: Well, Ralph, we were e-mailed a link to an online tutorial that explains a lot of the core functions and abilities of the new system.

M: ① <u>I saw that, but I doubt it could really help me. I usually learn best through in-person training... not through Web resources.</u>

W-1: I see what you're saying, but I've taken this tutorial myself. It's not just text, but demonstration videos and exercises with audio features.

M: That does sound helpful. Theresa, have you tried it?

W-2: Yes, and I agree with Ellen that it explains the new software very well. After about just 20 minutes, ② <u>I felt comfortable doing everything with the system... including complex operations like monthly reporting.</u>

W-1: That's true. As a matter of fact, I was able to get those kinds of assignments done... I'd say... about 30 percent faster than usual.

W-2: I feel the same way, and that procedure is also well-explained in the tutorial.

M: I think you've both convinced me. I'll go online and try it out.

對話內容中譯

59到61題題目與以下三人之間的對話有關。

男：艾倫，我有點難理解這個昨天新安裝的會計系統。你呢？

女一：這個嘛，拉爾夫，我們有收到電子郵件，裡面有線上教學的連結，解釋許多新系統的核心運作和功能。

男：①我有看到，但是我懷疑那真的能幫到我。我通常是透過面對面訓練學的最好的……而不是透過網路資源。

女一：我懂你的意思，但是我有自己用過這教學。它並不只是文字而已，還有示範影片和附有聲音功能的練習。

男：那聽起來確實很有幫助。特瑞莎，你有試過了嗎？

女二：有的，而且我同意艾倫，它真的把新軟體解釋得很清楚。大概在二十分鐘過後，②軟體用起來就很上手……包括像是月報的複雜操作。

女一：那是真的。事實上，我可以用……我會說……大概快30%的速度，完成工作。

女二：我也是這麼覺得，而且教學裡將流程講解得很清晰。

男：我想你們兩個已說服我了。我會上網試試看。

59. **Where most likely is the conversation taking place?**

(A) At an IT convention
(B) In a business office
(C) In a computer store
(D) At a systems seminar

237

59. 對話最有可能在哪個地方發生？

(A) 資訊科技會議

(B) 商業辦公室

(C) 電腦商店

(D) 系統研討會

正確答案 **(B)**

　　本題為提示會出現好幾次的類型。3人正針對安裝新的會計軟體進行對話。由於提示會出現數次，所以就算錯過了最初的提示還是能夠作答。如果在開頭部分覺得自己「好像已經漏聽提示」的話，就等60和61答完後再回頭圈選這題。另外，對於刪去法這類題目也很管用。

---

60. What does Ralph suggest about the software?

(A) It appears to be complex.

(B) It lacks any online tutorial.

(C) It has to be installed soon.

(D) It has to use audio features.

60. 拉爾夫針對軟體題出了什麼建議？

(A) 它看起來很複雜。

(B) 它缺少線上教學。

(C) 它需要盡快安裝。

(D) 它需要使用聲音功能。

正確答案 (A)

題目中出現了Ralph這個專有名詞，所以聽的時候就要多注意聽Ralph。起初女性用Well, Ralph和對方打招呼，所以可以得知對話開頭詢問「有點難理解這昨天安裝的新會計系統，你呢？」的男性就是Ralph。在底線①男性第2次的發言中，他回說「有看到，但是我懷疑那真的能幫到我。我通常是透過面對面訓練學的最好的……而不是透過網路資源」，因此可得知正確答案為(A)。題目中用了suggest這字，所以答案可以用推測的。

......

61. **What do the women say about monthly reporting?**
   (A) It uses up too many resources.
   (B) It requires better software.
   (C) Its operational speed has been affected.
   (D) Its usual content has been taken offline.

題目及選項中譯

61. 關於月報，女子說了什麼？
   (A) 它使用掉太多資源。
   (B) 它需要更好的軟體。
   (C) 它的運作速度有受到影響。
   (D) 它之前的內容已被撤離線。

正確答案 (C)

關鍵字是monthly reporting，在對話中應該會出現monthly reporting或是相同意思的其他說法。底線②的「女性2」的發言中就出現了monthly reporting，那之後「女性1」提到「事實上，我可以用……我會說……大概快30%的速度，完成工作。」，因此將這部分換句話說的(C)就是正確答案。

62-64　　　　　　　　　　　　　 80

The next three questions, 62 to 64 relate to the following conversation and graphic.

🇦🇺 W 🇨🇦 M

W: ① I'm calling about a lamp that I bought from your store. I'm using the assembly guide to put it together, but I think I'm missing a piece.

M: I'm very sorry to hear that. Could you please tell me what it is?

W: Well, ② I have the stand and both arms, but the other main piece is missing.

M: I can understand how that would be a problem. I can have one sent out to your address, and it would arrive in 3 to 5 business days.

解答和解析

PART 1 照片描述

PART 2 應答問題

PART 3 簡短對話

PART 4 簡短獨白

TOEIC聽力測驗 預想模擬試題

W: Can't it be sent any faster? I'd like to put this thing together as soon as possible.

M: I understand. ③ I'll have the item sent overnight.

對話內容中譯

62到64題題目與以下對話及圖表有關。

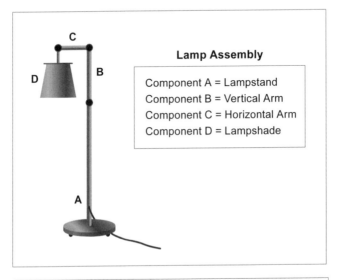

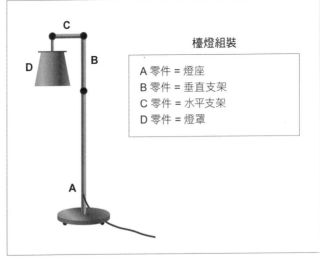

女：①<u>我來電是想詢問我在你們店裡買的一盞檯燈的事情。我正在使用組裝教學把檯燈組合起來，但是我認為我少了一塊零件。</u>

男：我非常抱歉聽到這件事。你可以告訴我是哪一塊嗎？

女：這個嘛，②<u>我有支撐架和兩邊的支架，但是另一個主要的零件不見了。</u>

男：我明白問題在哪了。我可以將該零件寄去你的地址，但是大概會需要三到五個工作天才會到達。

女：不能更快嗎？我想要盡快把它組裝好。

男：我懂。③<u>我會讓它隔夜送達。</u>

....

62. **Where does the man most likely work?**

    (A) In sales
    (B) In planning
    (C) In customer service
    (D) In IT

題目及選項中譯

62. 男子最有可能在哪裡工作？

    (A) 銷售
    (B) 企劃
    (C) 顧客服務
    (D) 資訊科技

正確答案　(C)

　　本題為提示會出現好幾次的題目。雖然提示會出現數次，但還是請在知道答案時就早點圈選好答案。起初女性提到「我來電是想詢問我在你們店裡買的一盞檯燈的事情。我正在使用組裝教學把檯燈組合起來，但是我認為我少了一塊零件」（底線①），由此可得知這是買了商品的客人與店員之間透過電話進行的對話，因此正確

答案為(C)。

....

63. **Look at the graphic. What component is the woman missing?**

(A) Component A
(B) Component B
(C) Component C
(D) Component D

題目及選項中譯

63. 請看圖表。女子缺少的零件為何？

(A) A 零件
(B) B 零件
(C) C 零件
(D) D 零件

正確答案　(D)

　　底線②的地方女性提及「我有支撐架和兩邊的支架，但是另一個主要的零件不見了」，因此可得知少的是(D) Lampshade（燈罩）。作圖表題時，在播放對話前先仔細確認過圖表的內容這件事相當重要。

....

64. **When will the woman receive the component?**

(A) In one day
(B) In three days
(C) In five days
(D) In seven days

題目及選項中譯

64. 女子什麼時候會收到零件？

(A) 一天內
(B) 三天內
(C) 五天內
(D) 七天內

正確答案　(A)

　　最後男性說「我會讓它隔夜送達」（底線③），所以正確答案為(A)。overnight（【副】一整夜地【形】一整夜的）是TOEIC的重要單字，日常生活中也經常用到，若不知道overnight的意思就答不出這題。

注釋

☐ assembly 組裝
☐ component 零件
☐ verticle 垂直的
☐ horizontal 水平的
☐ lampshade 燈罩
☐ put~together 將～組合在一起
☐ business day 工作天
☐ overnight 一整夜地
☐ customer service 顧客服務

65-67

 81

The next three questions, 65 to 67 refer to the following conversation and chart.

🇬🇧 M 🇺🇸 W

M: Have you read the new sales report?

W: I have, and ① <u>I must say I was disappointed to see what product sold the worst.</u>

M: Because we had provided so much marketing support for it?

W: Exactly. After all, we gave far less support to our dining room furniture sets, and as you can see from this chart, they sold far better.

M: ② <u>It's difficult to anticipate these kinds of things.</u> I'm hoping that our entire line of products can experience higher sales next quarter.

W: You're right. ③ <u>I'm having a team meeting on Friday to examine several proposals to achieve that as well as more cost control.</u>

對話內容中譯

65到67題題目與以下對話及圖表有關。

男：你讀了新的銷售報告了嗎？

女：我讀了，而且①<u>我必須說，看到是哪個產品賣得最差，我感到很失望。</u>

男：因為我們提供了非常多行銷資源給它？

女：沒錯。畢竟，我們給飯廳家俱組的支援少非常多，但是你也可以從這個報表中看出，它們還賣得好得多。

男：②<u>這種事情很難預測。</u>我希望我們整條生產線可以在下一季得到更高的銷售數字。

女：你説的對。③<u>我這週五將參加一場團隊會議，會檢查幾個提案來達到這個目標和多一點的預算控制。</u>

65. Look at the graphic. What product is the woman disappointed about?

(A) Living room sets
(B) Dining room sets
(C) Bedroom furniture
(D) Kitchen cabinets

題目及選項中譯

65. 請看圖表。女子感到失望的是哪個產品？

(A) 客廳套組
(B) 飯廳套組
(C) 寢室傢俱
(D) 廚房櫥櫃

正確答案 **(C)**

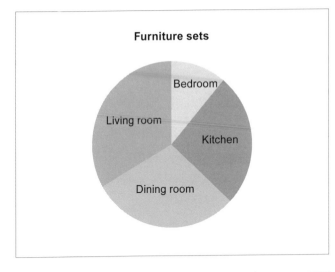

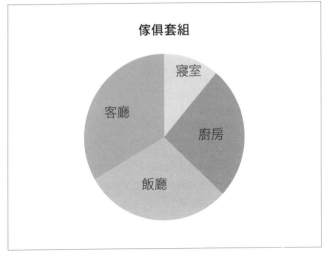

　　本題是關於圖表的題目。底線①的部分女性說到「我必須說，看到是哪個產品賣得最差，我感到很失望」，從圓餅圖上可看出銷售額最差的是寢室傢俱，因此正確答案為(C)。

66. What does the man say is very difficult?

(A) Testing products
(B) Forming a team
(C) Making forecasts
(D) Hiring more staff

題目及選項中譯

66. 男子說什麼事情非常困難？

(A) 測試產品
(B) 組成團隊
(C) 做預測
(D) 雇用更多員工

正確答案 (C)

底線②的部分男性表示「這種事情很難預測」，由此可得知正確答案為(C)。

....

67. What is indicated about the Friday meeting?

(A) It will consider ways to manage costs.
(B) It will examine human resources operations.
(C) It will combine groups from several departments.
(D) It will include a quarterly review of performances.

題目及選項中譯

67. 關於星期五的會議，何事有被指出？

(A) 思考控制預算的方法。
(B) 檢視人資營運。
(C) 結合來自不同部門的團隊。
(D) 包含績效的季審查。

解答和解析

PART 1 照片描述

PART 2 應答問題

PART 3 簡短對話

PART 4 簡短獨白

TOEIC聽力測驗 預想模擬試題

正確答案 (A)

關鍵字是Friday meeting。女性在最後的發言（底線③）中提到「我這週五將參加一場團隊會議，會檢查幾個提案來達到這個目標和多一點的預算控制」，所以正確答案為(A)。

注釋

- □ furniture 傢俱
- □ sales report 銷售報告
- □ be disappointed to 對～感到失望
- □ provide 提供
- □ anticipate 預測
- □ examine 檢查、檢視
- □ A as well as B A 連同 B
- □ form 形成
- □ quarterly 每季地
- □ after all 畢竟
- □ quarter 一季
- □ proposal 提案
- □ make a forecast 做預測

68-70

The next three questions, 68 to 70 relate to the following conversation and coupon.

🇨🇦 M 🇦🇺 W

M: Hi, I'd like to buy these 3 cases of yogurt. I've got a coupon for them.

W: OK, I'll just scan it into our system...oh, I'm sorry, but ① there's a problem. Do you see the restriction?

M: I hadn't noticed that until now. What do you suggest I do?

W: This coupon hasn't expired...so... uh...you could still get some use out of it.

M: Yes... but I really had my mind set on all of these cases... uh... since ② they're my favorite brand. ③ Would it be possible to get more of these coupons?

W: ④ Try our customer service desk at the rear of the store. Sometimes, they've got sheets of coupons like these.

對話內容中譯

62到64題題目與以下對話及優惠券有關。

男：嗨，我想要買這三盒優格。我有一張優惠券。

女：好的，我來將它掃描至我們的系統……噢，我很抱歉，但是①有個問題。你有看到限制嗎？

男：我現在才注意到。你建議我怎麼做？

女：這個優惠卷還沒有過期……所以……呃……你還是可以多少用到它。

男：是的……但是我真的決定要買這幾盒……呃……因為②它們是我最喜歡的牌子。③有可能再給我幾張這些優惠券嗎？

女：④去店後方的顧客服務櫃台問問看。有時候，他們有好幾張這種優惠券。

---

68. **Look at the graphic. Why is the coupon rejected?**

    (A) Because of the brands selected

    (B) Because of the number of cases

    (C) Because of the expiration date

    (D) Because of state limits

Balano Foods

DISCOUNT COUPON

15% off

Yogurt (all brands)

Limit: 1 case

Expiration date: March 31

Usable in all states nationwide

巴藍諾食品

折扣優惠券

85 折

優格（不限品牌）

限制：一盒

過期日：3/31

全國各州皆可使用

題目及選項中譯

68. 請看圖表。為什麼優惠券不能用？

(A) 因為有限定品牌

(B) 因為有限制盒數

(C) 因為過期了

(D) 因為有州際限制

正確答案 (B)

　　需在播放對話前先確認過優惠券的資訊，此時可初步推測出優惠券不能使用的原因，可能在於限制1盒的部分，或是有效期限的部分，然後在此之上去聽對話內容。男性拿出優惠券說想買3盒，之後在底線①的地方女性（店員）表示「有個問題。你有看到限制嗎？」看了優惠券後，合乎男性情況的限制事項只有Limit: 1 case（限制：一盒）而已，所以正確答案為(B)。

- -

69. **What does the man say about the yogurt?**

   (A) **He has considered it to be a favorite item.**
   (B) He has changed his mind about a restriction.
   (C) He needs to confirm the new retail price.
   (D) He wants to complain to store staff about it.

題目及選項中譯

69. 男子針對優格說了什麼？

   (A) 他認為這是他最喜歡的商品。
   (B) 關於一條限制他改變了主意。
   (C) 他需要確認新的零售價格。
   (D) 他想要向店員抱怨。

正確答案 (A)

　　題目寫說What does the man say ...，所以應該會是男性對於優格說了些什麼。底線②的地方男性提到「它們是我最喜歡的牌子。」由此可得知正確答案為(A)。

- -

70. **What most likely will the man do next?**

   (A) Choose a different food
   (B) Get more dishware sets

解答和解析

PART 1 照片描述

PART 2 應答問題

PART 3 簡短對話

PART 4 簡短獨白

TOEIC 聽力測驗 預想模擬試題

(C) Go to a customer service area

(D) Buy a sheet of postage stamps

【題目及選項中譯】

70. 男子接下來最有可能做何事？

(A) 選擇不同的食物

(B) 買更多餐具組

(C) 到顧客服務區

(D) 買一張郵票

正確答案 (C)

本題為第3小題經常出現的題型。題目使用了表示未來時態的 will，因此可推測出答案可能會在後半出現。底線③的地方男性問說「有可能再給我幾張這些優惠券嗎？」，對此女性在底線④的部分回說「去店後方的顧客服務櫃台問問看」，所以正確答案是(C)。

注釋

- limit 限制
- useable 可使用的
- restriction 限制
- get some use out of~ 多少使用～一點
- have one's mind set on~ 對於～心意已決
- at the rear of~ 在～的後方
- reject 拒絕
- retail price 零售價格
- postage stamp 郵票
- expiration date 到期日
- nationwide 全國性的
- expire 過期
- confirm 確認
- complain 抱怨

PART 4

The next three questions, 71 to 73 relate to the following radio broadcast.

M

And now for news from around the province. ① Barlen City School District is now holding its annual "Student Short Story Contest." ② Students aged 14 through 18 are encouraged to send in their entries. Stories should be no longer than 2,000 words and of course must be entirely written by the student. The winner of the contest will receive 100 euros' worth of gift certificates, as well as a trophy and a citation on the website of the district. ③ For more information or to submit an entry, go to www.westschooldistrict.edu.

獨白內容中譯

71到73題題目與以下電台廣播有關。

現在,讓我們來聽聽來自省各地的新聞。①巴冷市學區現在正在舉辦其年度的「學生小故事競賽」。②鼓勵年齡介於 14 到 18 歲的學生呈交作品。故事應低於 2000 字,且當然必須完全由該學生所撰寫。比賽的冠軍可以得到一百歐元的禮券、一個獎章,以及在地區網站上接受表揚。③想要獲得更多資訊,或是欲繳交作品,請至 www.westschooldistrict.edu.

71. What is the radio broadcast about?

(A) A competition
(B) A job opening
(C) An education course
(D) A teaching policy

題目及選項中譯

71. 廣播報導是關於什麼？

(A) 一項競賽

(B) 一項職缺

(C) 一個教育課程

(D) 一項教學政策

正確答案　(A)

　　底線①的地方提到「巴冷市學區現在正在舉辦其年度的「學生小故事競賽」，因此可得知這是關於(A)「學生短篇小説競賽」的廣播節目。

72. What restriction is mentioned in the radio broadcast?

(A) Work experience

(B) Age limits

(C) Assignment topics

(D) Investment rules

題目及選項中譯

72. 廣播報導中提到何項限制？

(A) 工作經驗

(B) 年齡限制

(C) 作品主題

(D) 投資規範

正確答案　(B)

　　底線②的地方提到「鼓勵年齡介於 14 到 18 歲的學生呈交作品」，由此可得知受限的是年齡，所以正確答案為(B)。

73. Why are listeners directed to a website?

    (A) To buy gift certificates

    (B) To view trophies

    (C) To download stories

    (D) To turn in projects

題目及選項中譯

73. 為什麼聽眾要去造訪網站？

    (A) 購買禮卷

    (B) 閱覽獎章

    (C) 下載故事

    (D) 呈交作品

正確答案　(D)

　　底線③的部分提到「想要獲得更多資訊，或是欲繳交作品，請至 www.westschooldistrict.edu.」，因此造訪網站的理由是(D)「呈交作品」。

注釋

- province 省
- school district 學區
- hold 舉辦
- annual 年度的
- aged 年齡位於～
- be encouraged to do 鼓勵進行～
- send in 繳交、呈交
- entry 作品
- entirely 完整地
- ...'s worth of~ 相當於~的價值
- gift certificate 禮券
- citation 引用、表揚
- competition 比賽
- job opening 職缺
- restriction 限制
- direct + 人 + to 引導人到～
- turn in~ 提交～

74-76

The next three questions, 74 to 76 relate to the following speech.

▇▇ W

Good morning. ① <u>I want to welcome all of you shareholders to this conference. I'm Nancy Fields, Investor Relations manager</u>. Before I begin, I want to tell you a bit of good news... uh... ② <u>we've had a historic year in terms of profits</u>. This has been reflected in the rise of our stock price...something that you've likely already noticed and are hopefully likely all pleased about. ③ <u>This afternoon, you're going to have a chance to hear from some of the company officers</u>, including CEO Josh Gardner, who is going to give a broad outline of our vision going forward. You'll also hear from our COO, Mina Powers, and, lastly, ④ <u>Gary Brooks, our CFO</u>.

獨白內容中譯

74到76題題目與以下演講有關。

早安。①<u>我想要歡迎各位股東參加這場會議。我是南西‧菲爾德，投資者關係企業的經理</u>。在我開始之前，我想要告訴各位一個好消息……呃……②<u>我們在收益方面，今年是具歷史性的一年</u>。這已經透過股價上漲反應出來了……這你們應該也早已注意到，也為此感到開心。③<u>這個下午，你們將會有一個機會聆聽公司職員的報告</u>，包括執行長賈許‧加德納，他將會把我們的未來展望以概括的方式呈現出來。你們同時也會聽取來自營運長米娜‧鮑爾思，以及最後，④<u>首席財務官蓋瑞‧布魯克思</u>的報告。

74. Who most likely are the listeners?
- **(A) Company stock owners**
- (B) Financial regulators
- (C) New employees
- (D) Business reporters

題目及選項中譯

74. 誰最有可能是聆聽者？
- **(A) 公司股東**
- (B) 金融調解人員
- (C) 新員工
- (D) 商業記者

正確答案　(A)

開頭部分底線①的地方提到「我想要歡迎各位股東參加這場會議。我是南西‧菲爾德，投資者關係企業的經理」，由此可知這場演講的聽眾是(A)「公司股東」。

75. According to the speaker, what has the company achieved this year?
- (A) A rise in employee productivity
- (B) Favorable coverage in the news
- (C) Higher market share for the firm
- **(D) Record income for the business**

題目及選項中譯

75. 根據演講者，公司今年達成了什麼？
- (A) 員工產能的提升
- (B) 新聞的正向報導
- (C) 更高的市佔率

(D) 企業破紀錄的營收

正確答案　**(D)**

　　演講者說完「在我開始之前，我想要告訴各位一個好消息」之後，又在底線②的地方說「我們在收益方面，今年是具歷史性的一年」，所以將這部分換句話說的(D)就是正確答案。

....

76. Who will talk last?
(A) Nancy Fields
(B) Josh Gardner
(C) Mina Powers
(D) Gary Brooks

題目及選項中譯

76. 誰會是最後演説的人？
(A) Nancy Fields
(B) Josh Gardner
(C) Mina Powers
(D) Gary Brooks

正確答案　**(D)**

　　底線③的地方提到「這個下午，你們將會有一個機會聆聽公司職員的報告」然後在including後面接上員工的名字和職務，在lastly之後，最後被舉出名字的是首席財務官蓋瑞‧布魯克思（底線④），因此正確答案為(D)。

77-79

The next three questions, 77 to 79 relate to the following news report.

🇬🇧 M

① Plandar Technologies has announced it will be building a research and development lab right here in Koleville. As part of this, ② it will be recruiting from around the metropolitan area. ③ Jobseekers with backgrounds in IT, accounting and management are especially encouraged to apply. Other jobs will range from maintenance to customer service. The company will provide additional details on this in the coming weeks.

④ Mayor Sharon Katz welcomed the arrival of the firm, saying that it was in line with her efforts to attract businesses to the area and grow the local economy.

獨白內容中譯

77到79題題目與以下新聞報導有關。

①普嵐達科技公司已公告，其將在克洛村這建造一個研發實驗室。作為這個的一部份，②其將在都市區附近招募員工。③也特別鼓勵具有資訊科技、會計，以及管理背景的求職者提出申請。其他工作則涵蓋維修到客服。公司將會在接下來幾個禮拜提供更多細節。④莎朗・卡茲市長歡迎公司的到來，並表示這與她努力在地區招商和活絡地方經濟的努力一致。

---

77. What is the news report mainly about?

(A) Local political elections
(B) Shopping mall construction
(C) A new facility that is opening
(D) A company marketing strategy

題目及選項中譯

77. 這則新聞報導主要與何事相關？

(A) 當地政治選舉

(B) 建造商場

(C) 正準備開立的新工廠

(D) 公司的行銷策略

正確答案 (C)

　　本題為提示會出現好幾次的題型。開頭部分底線①的部分提到「普嵐達科技公司已公告，其將在克洛村這建造一個研發實驗室」，因此正確答案為(C)。就算漏聽這個地方，其他部分也還會有提示，所以沒聽到的話就最後再回頭選吧。

78. What is suggested about Plandar Technologies?

(A) It has applied for a number of new patents.
(B) It has encouraged the city to lower its taxes.
(C) It has numerous open career opportunities.
(D) It has a leading position in the IT industry.

題目及選項中譯

78. 關於普嵐達科技公司的何事可被推測？

(A) 它申請了許多專利。

(B) 它鼓勵城市降稅。

(C) 它擁有許多職缺機會。

(D) 它在資訊科技產業具有領先地位。

正確答案　(C)

　　底線②的部分先是提到「其將在都市區附近招募員工」，接著在底線③的地方又說到「也特別鼓勵具有資訊科技、會計，以及管理背景的求職者提出申請。其他工作則涵蓋維修到客服。」，因此正確答案為(C)。

79. According to the news report, what is a goal of Ms. Katz?

(A) Bringing additional firms to the area
(B) Adding more staff to the city government
(C) Recruiting more economists for planning
(D) Making a better effort to reach out to voters

題目及選項中譯

79. 根據新聞報導，卡茲小姐的目標為何？

(A) 招募更多企業到當地

(B) 替市政府增添更多員工

解答和解析

PART 1 照片描述

PART 2 應答問題

PART 3 簡短對話

PART 4 簡短獨白

TOEIC 聽力測驗 預想模擬試題

(C) 替計畫召集更多經濟學家

(D) 針對貼近選民做更多努力

正確答案 (A)

　　請注意聽題目中出現的專有名詞**Ms. Katz**。後半出現了她的名字**Mayor Sharon Katz**，接著在底線④的地方提到「莎朗‧卡茲市長歡迎公司的到來，並表示這與她努力在地區招商和活絡地方經濟的努力一致」，由此可知正確答案為(A)。

注釋

- □ announce 公告
- □ recruit 募集
- □ background 背景
- □ be encouraged to do 被鼓勵做～
- □ apply 申請
- □ range from A to B 範圍從 A 到 B
- □ additional 額外的
- □ be in line with 與～一致
- □ attract 吸引
- □ election 選舉
- □ facility 設施
- □ apply for 申請
- □ patent 專利
- □ encourage...to do 鼓勵～去做
- □ lower 使降低
- □ leading 具領導地位的
- □ economist 經濟學家
- □ voter 投票者

- □ lab 實驗室
- □ jobseeker 求職者
- □ accounting 會計

- □ coming 即將到來的
- □ effort 努力
- □ business 企業、商業
- □ construciton 建造
- □ strategy 策略
- □ a number of 有一些

- □ numerous 許多的
- □ firm 企業
- □ reach out to~ 與～接觸

The next three questions, 80 to 82 relate to the following advertisement.

W

① At Jorno Bank, we work with all kinds of people to get them the loans they need to buy the house of their dreams. We specialize in working with people who may not have perfect credit or can make only low deposits. ② We work with potential borrowers to see if we can put together loan packages that are right for them, with manageable application expenses, interest rates, and monthly payments. Call or text message us today at 800-555-9050 to find out more. We'll try to put you into the home that you've always wanted. ③ Speak with one of our representatives today: the consultation itself is free.

獨白內容中譯

80到82題題目與以下廣告有關。

①在卓諾銀行，我們與形形色色的人們往來，並提供他們買夢想中的房子所需要的貸款。我們專攻沒有完美信用額度或是只能小額貸款的人士。② 我們與潛在的借方互動，透過合理的申請費用、利率，以及月費，確認我們是否可以替他們組合出一個適合他們的貸款方案。今天，來電或是傳簡訊至 800-555-9050 以取得更多訊息。我們會盡力幫您找到完美的住宅。③與我們的代理人來場今日談話：諮詢免費。

....

80. What is being advertised?

(A) **A mortgage provider**
(B) An accounting firm
(C) A real estate agency
(D) A debt collection business

題目及選項中譯

80. 廣告是關於什麼？
- **(A) 抵押借款商**
- (B) 會計公司
- (C) 房地產公司
- (D) 催債公司

正確答案 (A)

　　開頭部分底線①的地方提到「在卓諾銀行，我們與形形色色的人們往來，並提供他們買夢想中的房子所需要的貸款。我們專攻沒有完美信用額度或是只能小額貸款的人士」，所以正確答案為(A)。mortgage這個單字的意思是「抵押借款」，在日常生活中也經常用到。

....

81. According to the speaker, why would listeners choose this business?
- (A) Its loans are large.
- (B) Its service is fast.
- (C) Its record is perfect.
- **(D) Its fees are reasonable.**

題目及選項中譯

81. 根據說話者，為什麼聽眾要選擇它們的公司？
- (A) 它的貸款很多
- (B) 它的服務很快速
- (C) 它的紀錄很完美
- **(D) 它的費用合理**

正確答案 (D)

底線②的部分提到「我們與潛在的借方互動，透過合理的申請費用、利率，以及月費，確認我們是否可以替他們組合出一個適合他們的貸款方案」，因此將這部分換句話說的(D)即是正確答案。

---

82. What special offer is being made?
   (A) Deposits are unnecessary.
   (B) Packages arrive at no cost.
   (C) Consultations are for free.
   (D) Accounts are set up immediately.

題目及選項中譯

82. 提供了什麼特別優惠？
   (A) 無需押金
   (B) 免運費
   (C) 免費諮詢
   (D) 自動建立的帳戶

正確答案　(C)

　　最後在底線③的地方說到「與我們的代理人來場今日談話：諮詢免費」，由此可得知正確答案為(C)。

注釋

☐ specialize in 專攻　　　　☐ credit 信用額度
☐ deposit 存款；保證金；押金；定金
☐ potential 有潛力的
☐ put together~ 組合；拼裝起來
☐ loan package 貸款方案
☐ manageable 可管理的；易辦的；可應付的
☐ application 應用；申請

☐ expense 費用   ☐ interest rate 利率

☐ monthly payment 月支付款項

☐ find out~ 發現；找出

☐ representative 代理人；代表

☐ consultation 諮詢；商議

☐ free 免費的；自由的

☐ mortgage 抵押；抵押借款

☐ accounting firm 會計事務所

☐ real estate 不動產

☐ debt collection 收債；討債

☐ record 紀錄；記載   ☐ fee 服務費；費用

☐ reasonable 合理的   ☐ package 包裹

☐ account 帳戶   ☐ set up~ 建立；開創

83-85   🎧 88

The next three questions, 83 to 85 relate to the following talk.

🇺🇸 W

Before you all go to lunch, just listen up for a few minutes. ① <u>Work crews have been busy around our headquarters lately, upgrading lighting, doing painting and tile removal and replacement. Tomorrow, they're going to start on the plumbing system.</u> As a result, we won't have water on our floor from about 10 o'clock to 12 o'clock. If you're in the employee lounge, you won't be able to pour water, or make coffee or tea. The water will still be on for lower floors and the lobby, so you should go there if you... ah... er... get thirsty in the morning. Or, ② <u>as an alternative, you know, you can bring in your own bottled water from home.</u> ③ <u>This is something that we just have to get through.</u> If this is an issue for any of you, please let me know.

83到85題題目與以下獨白有關。

　　在你們去吃午餐之前，請聽我説話幾分鐘。①總部的工作團隊最近相當忙碌，忙著升級燈光、油漆，以及磁磚拆除和替換。明天，他們將要開始著手配管系統。因此，在十點到十二點之間，我們這層樓不會有用水。如果你在員工休息室的話，你將無法倒水，或是泡咖啡或茶。在較低樓層或是大廳還是會有用水，所以如果你早上渴了的話，可以去那裡。或者，②另外一個選擇是，你知道的，你可以從家裡帶自己的罐裝水。③這是我們必定要度過的。如果這對你們任何一位來說是個問題的話，請讓我知道。

---

83. What does the woman say has been taking place around the headquarters recently?

  (A) The performance of renovation projects
  (B) The expansion of some building areas
  (C) The replacement of some old equipment
  (D) The improvement of office supplies

83. 女子提及近期總部在正在進行何事？

  (A) 維修工程的執行
  (B) 某些大樓區域的擴建
  (C) 舊設備的更替
  (D) 辦公器具的改善

正確答案　(A)

　　底線①的部分提到「總部的工作團隊最近相當忙碌，忙著升級燈光、油漆，以及磁磚拆除和替換。明天，他們將要開始著手水管系統」，由此可得知最近總公司正在進行的事情是(A)「維修工程的執行」。

解答和解析

PART 1 照片描述

PART 2 應答問題

PART 3 簡短對話

PART 4 簡短獨白

TOEIC聽力測驗 預想模擬試題

84. What does the woman advise the listeners to do?

(A) Avoid some of the lower floors
(B) Bring in some items from home
(C) Meet later in the employee lounge
(D) Turn off the coffeemaker in the afternoon

題目及選項中譯

84. 女子建議聽眾做何事？

(A) 避免到低樓層
(B) 從家裡帶東西
(C) 晚點到員工休息室集合
(D) 下午關掉咖啡機

正確答案　(B)

　　在説了「在較低樓層或是大廳還是會有用水，所以如果你早上渴了的話，可以去那裡」之後，接著又説道「另外一個選擇是，你知道的，你可以從家裡帶自己的罐裝水」（底線②），所以正確答案為(B)。

85. What does the woman imply when she says, "This is something that we just have to get through"?

(A) A loss will be compensated for.
(B) A penalty will be endurable.
(C) A situation will be temporary.
(D) A business goal has to be reached.

85.當女子說「這是我們必定要度過的事情」時,她暗示著什麼?

(A) 損失將會有所賠償。

(B) 處罰是可以忍受的。

(C) 這個情況是暫時的。

(D) 企業目標必須達成。

正確答案 (C)

本題為詢問意圖題,這種題型必須從頭仔細聽,抓住話題整體的走向。以本題來說,最初在說目前正在進行裝修工程,接著告訴大家因為工程的關係我們這層從10點左右到12點會斷水,並暗示需要用水的人該採取怎樣的行動,之後表示 "This is something that we just have to get through"(這是我們必定要度過的事情時)(底線③)。因此,正確答案為(C)。題目中用了imply(暗示)這個字,所以答案可以用推測的。

注釋

- [ ] listen up 聆聽
- [ ] crew 團隊;一組工作人員
- [ ] headquaters 總部　　[ ] lately 近期
- [ ] upgrade 升級
- [ ] removal 移除;移動
- [ ] replacement 替代(物)
- [ ] plumbing 配管工程
- [ ] as a result 因此　　[ ] on 在~之上
- [ ] alternative 替代方案　　[ ] bring in~ 帶~進來
- [ ] bottled water 瓶裝水

□ get through 通過；完成
□ take place 發生；舉行
□ performance 表演；執行；性能
□ expansion 擴大；擴張
□ improvement 改善；改進
□ office supplies 辦公用品
□ turn off~ 關掉
□ compensate for~ 彌補　　□ penalty 處罰
□ endurable 耐用的　　□ temporary 暫時的

86-88

The next three questions, 86 to 88 relate to the following telephone message.

🇬🇧 M

① Hello, Ms. Chu, this is Brett Holden from Kazin Hotel. At the time of your reservation on our website, you indicated that you wanted us to contact you if any business suites became available during your planned stay. I'm happy to say that one now has. ② If you want to take advantage of this and upgrade, it would only cost you an additional 175 pounds a night. This would include a complimentary breakfast at our morning buffet, as well as two morning newspapers delivered to your door. Each of our suites also comes with a fax machine, scanner and printer...along with...uh...free wireless Internet. I've already sent you an e-mail, so you could just click on the links in it to make this change. Or you could call us back here at 800 – 555 – 9142. ③ We can only hold this room for you for the next two hours, so if you want it please call us back before then. Thank you, and have a nice day.

86到88題題目與以下電話留言有關。

①你好，朱小姐，我是卡辛飯店的布萊特霍登。在您於我們網站進行預約時，您表示若在您計劃的停留間有任何商務套房釋出，您希望我們聯絡您。我很高興通知您現在有一間空房。②若您想要利用此機會並升級，您每晚只需要多花 175 磅。這包含免費的自助式早餐，以及兩份送至您房間的晨報。我們每間套房皆附有傳真機、掃描和影印機，以及免費的無線網路。我已寄一封電子郵件給您，您可以透過連結進行更改。或者您也可以回撥這支電話 800-555-9142。③我們只能在接下來的兩個小時內替您保留這間房間，所以若您想要回電，請在那之前回撥。謝謝您，祝您有個愉快的一天。

......

86. Why is the man calling?

(A) To respond to an earlier customer request
(B) To promote a special seasonal sale at the business
(C) To confirm the upcoming arrival date of a guest
(D) To outline the dates still open for reservations

題目及選項中譯

86. 男子為什麼要打這通電話？

(A) 回應先前客戶的要求
(B) 宣傳公司的特別季節特賣
(C) 確認貴賓抵達的日期
(D) 概括仍能預約的日期

正確答案　(A)

　　打電話的目的大多會在開頭部分出現。底線①的地方提到「你好，朱小姐，我是卡辛飯店的布萊特霍登。在您於我們網站進行預約時，您表示若在您計劃的停留間有任何商務套房釋出，您希望我

們聯絡您。我很高興通知您現在有一間空房」，所以正確答案為 (A)。

87. Why would the listener have to pay an additional fee?

(A) **To receive an accommodations change**
(B) To have food and beverage room service
(C) To upgrade to faster wireless Internet service
(D) To have currency changed from dollars to pounds

題目及選項中譯

87. 為什麼聆聽者需要付額外的費用？

(A) 接受了住宿上的更改
(B) 擁有餐點和飲品的客房服務
(C) 升級至更快的無線網路服務
(D) 兌換美元至歐元

正確答案　(A)

底線①的地方先是傳達「你好，朱小姐，我是卡辛飯店的布萊特霍登。在您於我們網站進行預約時，您表示若在您計劃的停留間有任何商務套房釋出，您希望我們聯絡您。我很高興通知您現在有一間空房」這件事，接著又在底線說到「若您想要利用此機會並升級，您每晚只需要多花 175 磅」，因此將這個部分換句話說的(A)就是正確答案。

88. What does the man offer to do?

(A) Replace a broken printer
(B) Wait for a customer e-mail
(C) **Place a hold on a reservation**
(D) Call back within the next two hours

88. 男子提供什麼幫忙？

(A) 替換一個故障的影印機

(B) 等待客戶的電子郵件

(C) 預留房間預約

(D) 在接下來兩個小時內回電

正確答案 (C)

　　底線③的地方電話中的男性說到「我們只能在接下來的兩個小時內替您保留這間房間，所以若您想要回電，請在那之前回撥」，所以正確答案為(C)。

注釋

☐ reservation 保留；預約

☐ suite 套房

☐ take advantage of~ 趁機利用

☐ upgrade 升級

☐ complimentary 讚賞的；贈送的

☐ buffet 自助餐

☐ respond to~ 回應；答覆

☐ promote 促進；推廣

☐ confirm 證實；確認

☐ accommodation(s) 住宿

☐ currency 貨幣

☐ indicate 指示；表明

☐ available 可用的；有空的

☐ additional 附加的

☐ hold 保留

☐ request 要求；請求

☐ seasonal 季節性的

☐ outline 概述

解答和解析

PART 1 照片描述

PART 2 應答問題

PART 3 簡短對話

PART 4 簡短獨白

TOEIC 聽力測驗 預想模擬試題

89-91

 90

The next three questions, 89 to 91 relate to the following radio broadcast.

🇦🇺 W

Hi, I'm Leslie Blake reporting live from Ninth Avenue and Main Street downtown. ① <u>This area has been blocked off by the police for the filming of the new action movie</u>, Fire Wheels. This film, with an estimated production budget of 700 million dollars and some of the world's top stars, is already generating a lot of excitement. There are several dozen people gathered outside the security lines, hoping for a glimpse of some of the filming, and perhaps ② <u>the lead actor, Jessica Tan</u>. Filming will continue through Friday, so expect delays if you're driving through this neighborhood. ③ <u>Things here should be back to normal by Monday</u>.

獨白內容中譯

89到91題題目與以下電台廣播有關。

嗨，我是雷絲莉‧布雷克，在市中心第九大道和主街進行現場報導。①因拍攝新動作片《火輪》，警方已封鎖此區。這部預算約七億美元且卡司強大的電影，早已讓人們蠢蠢欲動。有數十人聚集在維安線外，希望能一睹拍攝內容的風采，以及②女主角潔西卡‧譚。拍攝會持續到週五，所以如果你要開車行經此社區的話，就可能會遇到延遲的狀況。③到週一就會回歸正常。

89. What is the radio broadcast mainly about?

(A) The use of a zone for a project
(B) The sales of a recent movie release
(C) The operations budget of a firm
(D) The winners of a theater award

275

89. 此廣播主要是關於什麼？

  (A) 一項計畫針對一塊區域的使用

  (B) 近期釋出的電影之票房

  (C) 電影預算的運作

  (D) 劇場獎的贏家們

正確答案　(A)

　　雖然會有點長，但本題得從開頭一路聽到中段才行。題示會出現好幾次，中段之前都要仔細聽，掌握住話題的走向。大街附近正在拍電影，為了電影的拍攝，警察將周遭封鎖，封鎖線外聚集著數十人，以上就是廣播內容的走向。此外，底線①提到「因拍攝新動作片……警方已封鎖此區」，因此可得知(A)為正確答案。(A)之中以a project這個說法來代換拍攝電影。

··

90. Who is Jessica Tan?

  (A) An athletic star

  (B) A police officer

  (C) A security consultant

  (D) An entertainer

90. 誰是潔西卡‧譚？

  (A) 運動明星

  (B) 警察

  (C) 維安顧問

  (D) 演藝人員

正確答案 (D)

關鍵字是Jessica Tan，只要有預先閱讀題目，就會發現必須注意去聽Jessica Tan。底線②提到「女主角潔西卡‧譚」，由此可得知她是正在拍攝中的這部電影的主角。因此，正確答案為(D)。

....

91. What does the woman mean when she says, "Things here should be back to normal by Monday"?

(A) Mondays are usually routine.
(B) An event will be over.
(C) A service will be complete.
(D) The crowds will be satisfied.

題目及選項中譯

91. 女子說「到週一就會回歸正常」是什麼意思？

(A) 星期一通常都是慣例性的。
(B) 一個活動將會結束。
(C) 一項服務將會完成。
(D) 群眾會感到滿意。

正確答案 (B)

說話者一直在說拍攝電影的事情，而快到「 」部分的時候提到「拍攝會持續到週五，所以如果你要開車行經此社區的話，就可能會遇到延遲的狀況」。考慮整個話題的走向，可得知 "Things here should be back to normal by Monday"（到週一就會回歸正常）（底線③）是在暗示星期一將會拍完，所以正確答案為(B)。

92-94

 91

The next three questions, 92 to 94 relate to the following talk.

🇬🇧 M

We've done reasonably well this year, but ① <u>next year we want to do even better</u>. To aid in this, we're going to be surveying our clients to better understand their core business needs. Currently, for example, we're almost entirely committed to developing and selling industrial goods.   ② <u>Our strategy department, however, feels that next year we might be able to earn significant revenues by focusing more on... ah... repairs and maintenance as well</u>. This could well be something both current and future customers would like to buy from us.   ③ <u>We want to establish whether this concept is truly realistic</u>. This survey will help us find out for sure.   ④ <u>When we get the results of the survey back... which will be in June</u>, we can go over them and then decide how we want to move forward.

獨白內容中譯

92到94題題目與以下獨白有關。

今年我們做得相當地不錯，但是①明年，我們想要做得更好。為了輔助這個想法，我們要開始訪問客戶以更佳了解他們的核心商業需求。舉例來說，近期，我們近乎全力投入於研發和販售工業產品上。②然而，我們的策略部門認為，明年我們可能可以同時藉由專注在……呃……維修和保養上，以賺取更多利潤。這可能是目前和未來客戶都會想要向我們購買的。③ 我們想確定這個想法可不可行，這份調查絕對能大大幫助我們。④等我們得到調查的回饋，也就是六月，就可以逐一檢視，然後再決定我們要怎麼接著進行。

....

92. What does the company want to focus on next year?

    (A) Committing to finding new staff

    (B) Developing new types of software

    (C) Surveying shopping mall customers

    (D) Entering potential new markets

題目及選項中譯

92. 公司明年想要專注於哪個方面？

    (A) 投入於尋找新客戶

    (B) 發展新型軟體

    (C) 調查商場的消費者

    (D) 進入潛在新市場

正確答案 (D)

關鍵字是next year，只要有預先閱讀題目，就會發現必須仔細去聽next year。底線①的地方提到next year we want to do even better（明年，我們想要做得更好），然後在後面一點說到「我們近乎全力投入於研發和販售工業產品上」，接著在底線②的地方更

進一步表示「然而，我們的策略部門認為，明年我們可能可以同時藉由專注在……呃……維修和保養上，以賺取更多利潤」，因此可得知正確答案即是將這部分換句話說的(D)。

....

93. What does the man imply when he says, "We want to establish whether this concept is truly realistic"?
- (A) A proposal is unlikely to be accepted.
- (B) Initial revenues are lower than expected.
- **(C) Research will verify the level of demand.**
- (D) Feedback from buyers has been limited.

題目及選項中譯

93. 當男子說「我們想確定這個想法可不可行」時，他暗示著什麼？
- (A) 提案不太可能被接受。
- (B) 最初的收入比預期還低。
- **(C) 調查會確立需求的程度。**
- (D) 消費者回饋已受到限制。

正確答案 (C)

　　本題為詢問意圖題，這種題型必須從開頭就仔細聽，並掌握住話題的走向。前半部分提到「為了進一步了解商業需求，將針對客戶進行調查」，之後又闡述「然而，我們的策略部門認為，明年我們可能可以同時藉由專注在……呃……維修和保養上，以賺取更多利潤」，在後面一點又說到 "We want to establish whether this concept is truly realistic" （底線③），考量話題整體的走向，可得知正確答案為(C)。題目中有imply（暗示）這個字，所以答案可以用推測的。

....

94. What will all of the listeners receive in June?

    (A) Lists of maintenance projects

    (B) Information about client needs

    (C) Results of ongoing repairs

    (D) Ideas on future production plans

題目及選項中譯

94. 在六月時，所有的聽眾都將收到什麼？

    (A) 維修專案的清單

    (B) 客戶需求的資訊

    (C) 現正進行中的維修之結果

    (D) 未來生產計畫的想法

正確答案　**(B)**

關鍵字是June，獨白中應該會出現June，記得要注意聽。後半部在底線④的地方提到When we get the results of the survey back ... which will be in June.（當我們得到調查的回饋，也就是六月），由此可得知正確答案為(B)。

注釋

☐ reasonably 合理地；相當地

☐ aid in 援救；幫助

☐ survey 調查

☐ currently 目前；現今

☐ be committed to doing 致力於做某事

☐ industrial goods 工業產品

☐ strategy 策略；戰略

☐ significant 有意義的；重大的

☐ revenue 收入

- ☐ focus on 集中
- ☐ as well 也
- ☐ establish 建造；設立；創辦
- ☐ realistic 實際可行的；現實的
- ☐ find out 發現；查明（真相）
- ☐ for sure 當然
- ☐ go over 查看；重溫
- ☐ potential 潛力
- ☐ proposal 提案；計畫
- ☐ be unlikely to do 不太可能做～
- ☐ initial 最初的；起初的
- ☐ verify 證實；證明
- ☐ ongoing 進行的；前進的

95-97

The next three questions, 95 to 97 relate to the following announcement and list.

W

I'm glad to see that everyone's here. I have an update on the catering system we've been using. ① To begin with, I want to remind you that only department managers like yourselves are permitted to order catering, and the expense for that comes out of your department budgets.　② From April 2, though, you'll need to order exclusively from one restaurant... uh... obviously one with delivery service. ③ The restaurant we finally choose will be the one with the best corporate discount. After that, you'll be able to just log onto an internal section of our Web site titled "catering." Follow the directions from there to place your order.　④ We're looking forward to this, because it's certain to be a big cost savings for us, as well as providing more efficiency.

獨白內容中譯

95到97題題目與以下公告有關。

我很高興看到大家都在這。針對我們使用的外燴系統，我有個最新消息。①首先，我想要提醒你們，只有像你們一樣的部門經理可以點餐飲系統，且該花費是來自於你部門的預算。②不過，從四月二日開始，你們只能從一間餐廳點餐……呃……很明顯就是可以外送的那間。③我們最終選擇的餐廳會是有最優惠企業折扣的那間。在那之後，你們就可以簡單地登入我們網站內部一個叫做「餐飲」的區塊。根據那邊的指示進行點餐。④我們非常期待，因為這對我們來說無疑省了一大筆錢，同時也提升了許多效率。

....

95. What does the speaker remind the listeners about?

(A) Department reorganizations
(B) System errors
(C) Authorization levels
(D) Manager bonuses

題目及選項中譯

95. 演講者提醒了聽眾何事？

(A) 部門整合

(B) 系統錯誤

(C) 授權級別

(D) 經理紅利

正確答案　(C)

底線①的地方提到「首先，我想要提醒你們，只有像你們一樣的部門經理可以點餐飲系統，且該花費是來自於你部門的預算」，所以正確答案為(C)。

RESTAURANTS WITH CATERING SERVICE	
Restaurant	Corporate Catering Discount
Paul's	10%
Everything Eats	12%
Wonder i-Chef	13%
Super Amaze	14%

提供外燴服務的餐廳	
餐廳	企業點餐折扣
Paul's	10%
Everything Eats	12%
Wonder i-Chef	13%
Super Amaze	14%

96. Look at the graphic. What restaurant will the company choose?

    (A) Paul's

    (B) Everything Eats

    (C) Wonder i-Chef

    (D) Super Amaze

題目及選項中譯

96. 請看圖表。公司會選擇哪間餐廳？

    (A) Paul's

    (B) Everything Eats

    (C) Wonder i-Chef

    (D) Super Amaze

解答和解析

PART1 照片描述

PART 2 應答問題

PART 3 簡短對話

PART 4 簡短獨白

TOEIC聽力測驗 預想模擬試題

正確答案 (D)

　　本題是與圖表有關的題目。在播放英文前預先確認選項時，會發現選項寫著餐廳的店名。因此可得知必須注意聽的是圖表上餐廳店名以外的項目，也就是折扣的部分。底線③的地方提到「我們最終選擇的餐廳會是有最優惠企業折扣的那間」，而餐廳之中折扣最多的就是(D) Super Amaze。

---

97. Why is the company looking forward to April 2?

(A) It will get exclusive product demands.

(B) It will have better website functionality.

(C) It will become more operationally efficient.

(D) It will improve the quality of its food.

題目及選項中譯

97. 為什麼公司期待四月二號的到來？

(A) 它會得到獨家的產品需求。

(B) 它的網站會擁有更佳的性能。

(C) 它的運作會更有效率。

(D) 它會改善其食物的品質。

正確答案 (C)

　　底線②提到「不過，從四月二日開始，你們只能從一間餐廳點餐」，而且最後在底線④的部分說「我們非常期待，因為這對我們來說無疑省了一大筆錢，同時也提升了許多效率。」，由這些地方可得知正確答案為(C)。

- discount 折扣
- update 更新
- to begin with 首先;第一
- remind + 人 + that 提醒某人某事
- be permitted to do 被允許做某事
- expense 費用
- exclusively 獨家地;專門地
- obviously 明顯地
- log onto~ 登錄
- internal 內部的;內在的
- follow the directions 按照指示
- place an order 訂購
- be looking forward to 期待
- certain 無疑的;確定的
- cost saving 成本節省
- efficiency 效率;效能
- reorganization 重新組織
- authorization 授權;認可
- bonus 獎金
- exclusive 獨有的;專用的
- functionality 機能
- operationally 操作上地
- efficient 有效率的

98-100

The next three questions, 98 to 100 relate to the following talk and map.

 M

Okay, it's about time to start our meeting. ① I want to start by discussing the location of our new distribution center, where our goods bought wholesale will be sorted and then shipped out to customers who buy from our website. Apart from the warehouses, we're also going to have a number of support facilities on the premises, such as human resources and retail operations and planning. We've been considering a number of areas as candidates for the center. We've settled on Albana County. ② It has 4 districts, and the board wants the one with easy and clear access to the rail line going through it. I know that's not as close as we'd like to Lake Lopona, but that's an unavoidable tradeoff. I'm going to first explain how this will be carried out. ③ At the end of the meeting today, I'm going to assign each of you to different groups responsible for different phases of this project.

獨白內容中譯

98到100題題目與以下獨白及地圖有關。

好的，我們該開始會議了。①我想要先從我們運輸中心的地點開始討論，這是我們以批發價購買之產品進行分類和派送給由網路下單的顧客之地。除了倉庫，我們在場址上同時也會有一些支援設施，像是人力資源、零售營運，以及企畫。我們已經針對此中心進行多個候選地點的考量。最終我們決定要設址在阿爾巴馬郡。②它總共有四個區，而董事會想要的是可以輕易清楚地接到穿過它的鐵軌的區域。我知道這和我們預想的洛坡那河區相去甚遠，但是這是無法避免的交涉。我將要先解釋這會怎麼進行。③在今天的會議過後，我會將各位指派到不同團隊，負責此專案的不同階段。

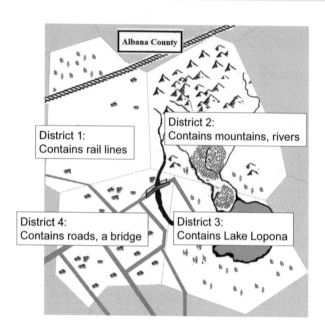

解答和解析

PART 1 照片描述

PART 2 應答問題

PART 3 簡短對話

PART 4 簡短獨白

TOEIC聽力測驗 預想模擬試題

98. Where does the speaker work?

   (A) At a government office
   (B) At a property management business
   (C) At an Internet retailer
   (D) At an asset management firm

題目及選項中譯

98. 說話者在哪裡工作？

   (A) 政府辦公室
   (B) 房地產管理企業
   (C) 網路零售
   (D) 資產管理公司

正確答案　(C)

    開頭部分要聽的內容稍長。底線①提到「我想要先從我們運輸中心的地點開始討論，這是我們以批發價購買之產品進行分類和派送給由網路下單的顧客之地」，所以正確答案為(C)。正式考試時，website和internet兩者經常會互相代換。

99. Look at the graphic. What district will be chosen?

   (A) District 1
   (B) District 2
   (C) District 3
   (D) District 4

題目及選項中譯

99. 請看圖表。哪一區將會中選？

   (A) 第一區
   (B) 第二區
   (C) 第三區
   (D) 第四區

正確答案 (A)

關於候補地，在底線②的地方提到「它總共有四個區，而董事會想要的是可以輕易清楚地接到穿過它的鐵軌的區域。我知道這和我們預想的洛坡那河區相去甚遠」。確認地圖後發現離鐵路較近的是District 1和District 2，但District 2那邊山很多不易去。另外，也提到該地離Lopona湖有段距離，所以也不是District 3或District 4。因此，(A) District 1即是正確答案。

....

100. What will the speaker do at the end of the meeting?

    (A) Assign people to teams
    (B) Take questions about plans
    (C) Finalize a relocation schedule
    (D) Contact the board of directors

題目及選項中譯

100. 演講者在會議結尾將會做何事？

    (A) 指派人員到團隊中
    (B) 接受關於計畫的問題
    (C) 將遷移計劃定案
    (D) 聯絡董事會

正確答案 (A)

題目中有at the end of the meeting，所以可推測出提示可能會出現在後半。底線③的地方提到「在今天的會議過後，我會將各位指派到不同團隊，負責此專案的不同階段」，因此正確答案為(A)。

注釋

- [ ] district 地區；地帶
- [ ] distribution center 配送中心
- [ ] wholesale 批發
- [ ] sort 分類；種類
- [ ] ship out to~ 出貨到
- [ ] apart from 除～之外
- [ ] warehouse 倉庫
- [ ] a number of~ 一些
- [ ] facility 技能；能力
- [ ] permises 場所、建物地基
- [ ] human resources 人力資源
- [ ] retail operation 零售運營
- [ ] candidate 候選人
- [ ] settle on~ 選擇；決定
- [ ] board 董事會
- [ ] rail line 鐵路線
- [ ] unavoidable 不可避免的
- [ ] tradeoff 交易
- [ ] carry out~ 執行；進行
- [ ] assign A to B 分配A給B
- [ ] property 財產；所有物
- [ ] retailer 零售商
- [ ] asset 資產
- [ ] finalize 完成；結束
- [ ] relocation 遷移
- [ ] board of directors 董事會

NOTE

聽力模擬試題答案卡

LISTENING SECTION

Part 1

No.	ANSWER
1	A B C D
2	A B C D
3	A B C D
4	A B C D
5	A B C D
6	A B C D
7	A B C
8	A B C
9	A B C
10	A B C

Part 2

No.	ANSWER	No.	ANSWER
11	A B C	21	A B C
12	A B C	22	A B C
13	A B C	23	A B C
14	A B C	24	A B C
15	A B C	25	A B C
16	A B C	26	A B C
17	A B C	27	A B C
18	A B C	28	A B C
19	A B C	29	A B C
20	A B C	30	A B C

No.	ANSWER
31	A B C
32	A B C D
33	A B C D
34	A B C D
35	A B C D
36	A B C D
37	A B C D
38	A B C D
39	A B C D
40	A B C D

Part 3

No.	ANSWER	No.	ANSWER
41	A B C D	51	A B C D
42	A B C D	52	A B C D
43	A B C D	53	A B C D
44	A B C D	54	A B C D
45	A B C D	55	A B C D
46	A B C D	56	A B C D
47	A B C D	57	A B C D
48	A B C D	58	A B C D
49	A B C D	59	A B C D
50	A B C D	60	A B C D

No.	ANSWER
61	A B C D
62	A B C D
63	A B C D
64	A B C D
65	A B C D
66	A B C D
67	A B C D
68	A B C D
69	A B C D
70	A B C D

Part 4

No.	ANSWER	No.	ANSWER	No.	ANSWER
71	A B C D	81	A B C D	91	A B C D
72	A B C D	82	A B C D	92	A B C D
73	A B C D	83	A B C D	93	A B C D
74	A B C D	84	A B C D	94	A B C D
75	A B C D	85	A B C D	95	A B C D
76	A B C D	86	A B C D	96	A B C D
77	A B C D	87	A B C D	97	A B C D
78	A B C D	88	A B C D	98	A B C D
79	A B C D	89	A B C D	99	A B C D
80	A B C D	90	A B C D	100	A B C D

聽力模擬試題答案卡

LISTENING SECTION

Part 1

No.	ANSWER A B C D
1	Ⓐ Ⓑ Ⓒ Ⓓ
2	Ⓐ Ⓑ Ⓒ Ⓓ
3	Ⓐ Ⓑ Ⓒ Ⓓ
4	Ⓐ Ⓑ Ⓒ Ⓓ
5	Ⓐ Ⓑ Ⓒ Ⓓ
6	Ⓐ Ⓑ Ⓒ Ⓓ
7	Ⓐ Ⓑ Ⓒ
8	Ⓐ Ⓑ Ⓒ
9	Ⓐ Ⓑ Ⓒ
10	Ⓐ Ⓑ Ⓒ

Part 2

No.	ANSWER A B C
11	Ⓐ Ⓑ Ⓒ
12	Ⓐ Ⓑ Ⓒ
13	Ⓐ Ⓑ Ⓒ
14	Ⓐ Ⓑ Ⓒ
15	Ⓐ Ⓑ Ⓒ
16	Ⓐ Ⓑ Ⓒ
17	Ⓐ Ⓑ Ⓒ
18	Ⓐ Ⓑ Ⓒ
19	Ⓐ Ⓑ Ⓒ
20	Ⓐ Ⓑ Ⓒ

No.	ANSWER A B C
21	Ⓐ Ⓑ Ⓒ
22	Ⓐ Ⓑ Ⓒ
23	Ⓐ Ⓑ Ⓒ
24	Ⓐ Ⓑ Ⓒ
25	Ⓐ Ⓑ Ⓒ
26	Ⓐ Ⓑ Ⓒ
27	Ⓐ Ⓑ Ⓒ
28	Ⓐ Ⓑ Ⓒ
29	Ⓐ Ⓑ Ⓒ
30	Ⓐ Ⓑ Ⓒ

Part 3

No.	ANSWER A B C D
31	Ⓐ Ⓑ Ⓒ
32	Ⓐ Ⓑ Ⓒ Ⓓ
33	Ⓐ Ⓑ Ⓒ Ⓓ
34	Ⓐ Ⓑ Ⓒ Ⓓ
35	Ⓐ Ⓑ Ⓒ Ⓓ
36	Ⓐ Ⓑ Ⓒ Ⓓ
37	Ⓐ Ⓑ Ⓒ Ⓓ
38	Ⓐ Ⓑ Ⓒ Ⓓ
39	Ⓐ Ⓑ Ⓒ Ⓓ
40	Ⓐ Ⓑ Ⓒ Ⓓ

No.	ANSWER A B C D
41	Ⓐ Ⓑ Ⓒ Ⓓ
42	Ⓐ Ⓑ Ⓒ Ⓓ
43	Ⓐ Ⓑ Ⓒ Ⓓ
44	Ⓐ Ⓑ Ⓒ Ⓓ
45	Ⓐ Ⓑ Ⓒ Ⓓ
46	Ⓐ Ⓑ Ⓒ Ⓓ
47	Ⓐ Ⓑ Ⓒ Ⓓ
48	Ⓐ Ⓑ Ⓒ Ⓓ
49	Ⓐ Ⓑ Ⓒ Ⓓ
50	Ⓐ Ⓑ Ⓒ Ⓓ

No.	ANSWER A B C D
51	Ⓐ Ⓑ Ⓒ Ⓓ
52	Ⓐ Ⓑ Ⓒ Ⓓ
53	Ⓐ Ⓑ Ⓒ Ⓓ
54	Ⓐ Ⓑ Ⓒ Ⓓ
55	Ⓐ Ⓑ Ⓒ Ⓓ
56	Ⓐ Ⓑ Ⓒ Ⓓ
57	Ⓐ Ⓑ Ⓒ Ⓓ
58	Ⓐ Ⓑ Ⓒ Ⓓ
59	Ⓐ Ⓑ Ⓒ Ⓓ
60	Ⓐ Ⓑ Ⓒ Ⓓ

Part 4

No.	ANSWER A B C D
61	Ⓐ Ⓑ Ⓒ Ⓓ
62	Ⓐ Ⓑ Ⓒ Ⓓ
63	Ⓐ Ⓑ Ⓒ Ⓓ
64	Ⓐ Ⓑ Ⓒ Ⓓ
65	Ⓐ Ⓑ Ⓒ Ⓓ
66	Ⓐ Ⓑ Ⓒ Ⓓ
67	Ⓐ Ⓑ Ⓒ Ⓓ
68	Ⓐ Ⓑ Ⓒ Ⓓ
69	Ⓐ Ⓑ Ⓒ Ⓓ
70	Ⓐ Ⓑ Ⓒ Ⓓ

No.	ANSWER A B C D
71	Ⓐ Ⓑ Ⓒ Ⓓ
72	Ⓐ Ⓑ Ⓒ Ⓓ
73	Ⓐ Ⓑ Ⓒ Ⓓ
74	Ⓐ Ⓑ Ⓒ Ⓓ
75	Ⓐ Ⓑ Ⓒ Ⓓ
76	Ⓐ Ⓑ Ⓒ Ⓓ
77	Ⓐ Ⓑ Ⓒ Ⓓ
78	Ⓐ Ⓑ Ⓒ Ⓓ
79	Ⓐ Ⓑ Ⓒ Ⓓ
80	Ⓐ Ⓑ Ⓒ Ⓓ

No.	ANSWER A B C D
81	Ⓐ Ⓑ Ⓒ Ⓓ
82	Ⓐ Ⓑ Ⓒ Ⓓ
83	Ⓐ Ⓑ Ⓒ Ⓓ
84	Ⓐ Ⓑ Ⓒ Ⓓ
85	Ⓐ Ⓑ Ⓒ Ⓓ
86	Ⓐ Ⓑ Ⓒ Ⓓ
87	Ⓐ Ⓑ Ⓒ Ⓓ
88	Ⓐ Ⓑ Ⓒ Ⓓ
89	Ⓐ Ⓑ Ⓒ Ⓓ
90	Ⓐ Ⓑ Ⓒ Ⓓ

No.	ANSWER A B C D
91	Ⓐ Ⓑ Ⓒ Ⓓ
92	Ⓐ Ⓑ Ⓒ Ⓓ
93	Ⓐ Ⓑ Ⓒ Ⓓ
94	Ⓐ Ⓑ Ⓒ Ⓓ
95	Ⓐ Ⓑ Ⓒ Ⓓ
96	Ⓐ Ⓑ Ⓒ Ⓓ
97	Ⓐ Ⓑ Ⓒ Ⓓ
98	Ⓐ Ⓑ Ⓒ Ⓓ
99	Ⓐ Ⓑ Ⓒ Ⓓ
100	Ⓐ Ⓑ Ⓒ Ⓓ

聽力模擬試題答案卡

LISTENING SECTION

Part 1

No.	ANSWER
1	A B C D
2	A B C D
3	A B C D
4	A B C D
5	A B C D
6	A B C D
7	A B C
8	A B C
9	A B C
10	A B C

Part 2

No.	ANSWER
11	A B C
12	A B C
13	A B C
14	A B C
15	A B C
16	A B C
17	A B C
18	A B C
19	A B C
20	A B C
21	A B C
22	A B C
23	A B C
24	A B C
25	A B C
26	A B C
27	A B C
28	A B C
29	A B C
30	A B C
31	A B C
32	A B C
33	A B C
34	A B C
35	A B C
36	A B C
37	A B C
38	A B C
39	A B C
40	A B C

Part 3

No.	ANSWER
41	A B C D
42	A B C D
43	A B C D
44	A B C D
45	A B C D
46	A B C D
47	A B C D
48	A B C D
49	A B C D
50	A B C D
51	A B C D
52	A B C D
53	A B C D
54	A B C D
55	A B C D
56	A B C D
57	A B C D
58	A B C D
59	A B C D
60	A B C D
61	A B C D
62	A B C D
63	A B C D
64	A B C D
65	A B C D
66	A B C D
67	A B C D
68	A B C D
69	A B C D
70	A B C D

Part 4

No.	ANSWER
71	A B C D
72	A B C D
73	A B C D
74	A B C D
75	A B C D
76	A B C D
77	A B C D
78	A B C D
79	A B C D
80	A B C D
81	A B C D
82	A B C D
83	A B C D
84	A B C D
85	A B C D
86	A B C D
87	A B C D
88	A B C D
89	A B C D
90	A B C D
91	A B C D
92	A B C D
93	A B C D
94	A B C D
95	A B C D
96	A B C D
97	A B C D
98	A B C D
99	A B C D
100	A B C D

NOTE

NOTE

原來如此 系列 E206

中村澄子老師的新制TOEIC聽力：
多益滿分全題型分析&必勝搶分模擬試題

有了這本多益閱讀考題高分秘笈，就算考題改制也不需擔心！

作　　　者　中村澄子（なかむら・すみこ）◎著
譯　　　者　費長琳、李思
顧　　　問　曾文旭
總 編 輯　王毓芳
編輯統籌　耿文國、黃璽宇
主　　　編　吳靜宜
執行主編　姜怡安
執行編輯　李念茨、陳儀蓁
美術編輯　王桂芳、張嘉容
法律顧問　北辰著作權事務所　蕭雄淋律師、幸秋妙律師

初　　　版　2019年08月
出　　　版　捷徑文化出版事業有限公司
電　　　話　（02）2752-5618
傳　　　真　（02）2752-5619
地　　　址　106 台北市大安區忠孝東路四段250號11樓-1

定　　　價　新台幣449元／港幣150元
產品內容　1書

總 經 銷　采舍國際有限公司
地　　　址　235 新北市中和區中山路二段366巷10號3樓
電　　　話　（02）8245-8786
傳　　　真　（02）8245-8718

港澳地區總經銷　和平圖書有限公司
地　　　址　香港柴灣嘉業街12號百樂門大廈17樓
電　　　話　（852）2804-6687
傳　　　真　（852）2804-6409

捷徑Book站

國家圖書館出版品預行編目資料

中村澄子老師的新制TOEIC聽力：多益滿分全題
型分析&必勝搶分模擬試題 / 中村澄子著. -- 初版.
-- 臺北市：捷徑文化, 2019.08
　　面；　公分（原來如此：E206）
ISBN 978-957-8904-87-3(平裝)

1. 多益測驗

805.1895　　　　　　　　　　　108009854

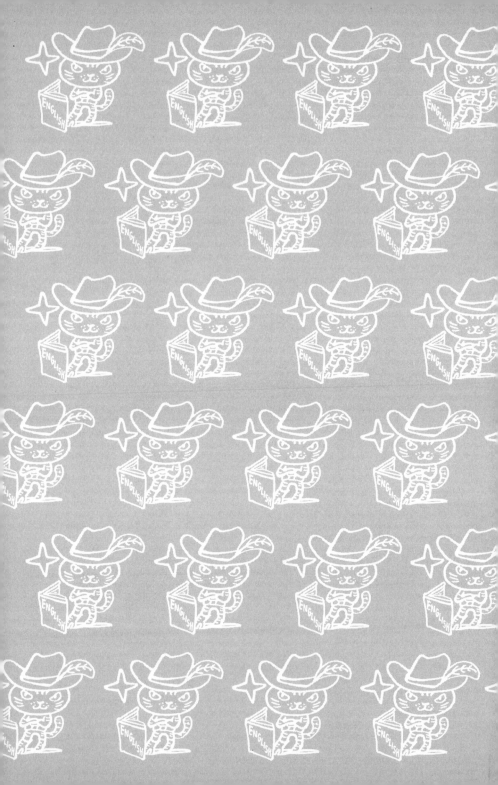